To all of the princesses out there—even if the tiara is invisible, or crooked.
- xoxo, Avery

Chapter One

Elle Olsen was either going to strangle him with his pine-colored silk tie or drag him into a dressing room and fuck his brains out. Too bad both options would get her fired right before her rent was due. Life was such a buzzkill that way.

The *him* in question was Dominick Rasmussen, one of the world's most eligible bachelors and the bane of her existence if she wanted to keep her job as head stylist at Dylan's. He'd walked onto the exclusive floor of the luxury department store accompanied by store CEO Devin Harris, who had told her to clear her calendar for the day and take very special care of an old friend in from London who needed a new winter wardrobe and then told her to enjoy her week in the sun—whatever that meant. The result had been several hours of trying to talk the sexy billionaire out of his black suit. Literally. The guy wouldn't try on anything that couldn't be accessorized by a Windsor knot.

"That is very—" He paused for a second, pursing his thick Tom Hardy–style lips together as he looked at the latest offering she held up, a soft wool fisherman's sweater in an indigo that would play off the icy Nordic hotness of his arctic-blue eyes and ash-blond hair, not to mention highlight his broad shoulders and superhero-level biceps. "Casual. I don't do casual."

Really? She totally hadn't been able to figure that out after his reaction when she showed him a pair of eight-hundred-dollar denim jeans. But a man couldn't live in only suits and the occasional tux—not even an international financier who spent as much time in the society pages as he did the boardroom. A wardrobe needed variety, it needed color, it needed to adapt. "Do you sleep in your suits, too?"

He dragged his gaze from the sweater she held up to her and completed a slow perusal starting at her totally reasonable three-and-a-half-inch metallic silver heels, up her bare calves, across the fitted pear-green pencil skirt, over her winter-white cashmere sweater and stopping briefly on her lips before reaching her eyes. She'd been stark naked, pressed up against a sixteenth-floor window, having one of the best orgasms of her life from a lover's tongue and hadn't been as turned on as she was at that moment. Fire licked its way across her skin, flicking at all of her sensitive spots until her entire body vibrated.

"Do I sleep in my suits? Do you really want to know?" he asked, his voice low with just enough dominating arrogance in it to make her shiver.

Electricity sparked in the air around them, obvious enough she could practically smell smoke in the air. She bit her bottom lip. Hard. Moaning out loud would be so bad right now. Fucking a Dylan's personal shopping client would be out of bounds. Spontaneously combusting from lust would be a total no-no. Of course, none of that made her want to do it any less. But what she needed was to not get fired from her job because she'd schtupped a client in full view of the discreet video cameras placed around the showroom.

"I'm sorry, that was an inappropriate question." Inhaling a deep breath, Elle forced her face into a mask of subservient neutrality so distant from her true nature. "It won't happen again, Mr. Rasmussen."

"Not Mr. Rasmussen. Call me Dom. I really think we should be on a first-name basis, since you know that I strip off my suit every night and get into bed wearing nothing at all."

Just like that, her panties became a lost cause. He grinned as if he knew she was picturing his muscular body sliding between crisp, white sheets. Tall, hard, and—like the Viking raiders she grew up hearing stories about—dangerous. It radiated from him like a tractor beam pulling her closer.

"Now tell me what you sleep in," he teased. "It's only fair."

"Life isn't fair." Especially not when the cool dismissal she'd meant to project got hijacked by that breathy I'm-so-frickin'-turned-on lilt to her voice.

"No, it's not." He reached out and twisted a strand of her wavy strawberry blond hair around his long finger. "That's why you have to make it bend to your will."

According to the tabloids, he liked to bend women over any available surface and fuck them brainless. Considering she'd lost about a gazillion IQ points from spending thirty minutes with him while completely dressed, she could imagine how many she'd lose if they were both naked. The image to accompany that thought flashed into her head, and her knees almost buckled. She had to get out of here before she said fuck the cameras and yanked him to the nearest horizontal surface.

"If you'll excuse me for a moment, I'll go find a few more options for you to consider." Elle hustled out of the showroom as fast as possible without looking like she was running for cover, which she totally was.

The staff-only area on the exclusive eighth floor of

Dylan's didn't have the chandeliers, plush sitting area, chilled champagne, and floor-to-ceiling mirrors the personal shopping showroom did, but she wouldn't have traded a single plastic chair or cup of hours-old coffee at that point for all that luxury. Instead, she sucked in the Dom pheromone–free air like a woman who'd just finished a triathlon while wearing one of those fake pregnancy bellies. Insta-lust had her by the metaphorical balls, and she needed a moment to get a hold of herself.

"Come on, girlie," Elle said to herself. "He's only a guy."

"Hey, Elle." Jaqui Shardwell, the only other personal shopper working on a Monday afternoon, peeked her head of her office. "You okay?"

Nope. Not even a little. "I'm good, just dealing with a client who doesn't like anything."

"Ugh. I feel your pain." She rolled her eyes in commiseration. "Remember that socialite who only wanted to wear puce retro sexy secretary dresses and fishnets?"

The memory of Carla Silbretti's brownish-purple phase had Elle giggling, relieving the tension stringing her body tight.

Jaqui's lips twisted, and she clasped her hands together. "Hey, I got a call from Halston's school. He threw up in the middle of class. I hate to ask, but…"

"Don't even think about it." She waved her colleague off. "Go get the little guy. We don't have any other clients scheduled for today, and if it gets crazy, I'll call in Rebecca from lingerie. She's been dying to audition for a spot up here since she earned her fashion degree."

Jaqui grabbed her purse, and they both headed toward the special elevator that led straight to the parking lot for the personal shopping customers who liked their anonymity. They were the same ones who decreed there could be no cameras near the elevators and got management to turn off the security cameras in the showroom so that no leaked photos of them wearing an unflattering outfit could ever get out.

"You are the best, thank you." Jacqui gave her a quick air kiss before the elevator doors closed.

Not for the first time, a pang of loneliness hit her. Mr. Icy Hot would be gone soon, and then it would be her in the showroom until closing…alone. Then she'd go home to her cute little one-bedroom apartment, where she'd binge on Netflix…alone. Finally she'd curl up for the night under a mountain of blankets…alone.

Friends hadn't been a possibility since she'd been abandoned in Harbor City at the ripe old age of seventeen. She couldn't risk letting anyone get close enough to discover her secret, so she'd compensated by working as much as possible, which allowed her to get her people fix and socialize, if only in a limited way. Boyfriends had been out, too, but she alleviated that need with her battery-operated boyfriend and infrequent, short-term lovers who never got the chance to know the real her. It wasn't the life she'd chosen, it wasn't the life her father would have chosen for her, but neither of them had been given a choice. When her world had blown up, the only option had been to run, to hide, to survive, so that's what she'd done.

"Elle," Dom said from behind her.

She whipped around to face him. What was he doing in the employee-only area? *What do you think, dumb ass? Parcheesi?*

He stood so close that the now-familiar tingling attraction snapped across her skin. He held one hand behind him, and the other reached for her, cupping the back of her head, his fingers tangling in her long hair. Oh, God, he was going to kiss her, and damn her mutinous body, she wanted him to. This was bad, but she'd lost her ability to care.

"Dom—"

The rest of the sentence was smothered by the white cotton cloth he held in his free hand and forced against her nose and mouth. Shock froze her to the spot. She couldn't blink. She couldn't breathe. All she could do was feel the banging of her heart as panic sent it into overdrive. The people who killed her family had found her.

"This is for your own good," he said as he looked down at her. "I couldn't take the chance you'd fight me, and there isn't time to explain."

Too damn bad for him, because her fight-or-flight response zinged into action. Whatever was in the cloth, she didn't want to breathe it in. Adrenaline clawed at her, demanding life-giving oxygen, but she refused to give in. They might have murdered everyone she loved and sent her into hiding, but she wouldn't go down without a fight. She grabbed his arms, yanking and stabbing her nails into the sliver of his wrists not covered by his shirt. He didn't flinch.

Dom kept his cold gaze on her, a icy determination making them even bluer somehow. "Just relax and breathe."

Fat fucking chance. Holding on to his forearms for leverage, she slammed her knee upward, aiming for his most vulnerable spot. He deflected the move with an ease of a natural athlete or a man trained to do whatever it took to force the world to do his bidding.

She fought against him, kicking and hitting, but he kept the cloth pressed against her nose and mouth. Her lungs burned with the effort not to breathe as she struggled in his iron grasp, but it didn't do her any good. Blackness ate around the edges of her vision, the lack of oxygen taking its toll. She didn't have long before she'd pass out, with or without the help of whatever chemical was in the cloth.

Ten years. She'd made it a decade without anyone finding her, without her secret coming out. Foolishly, she'd thought she was finally safe. Now she'd pay the price for a crown she'd never worn and a kingdom she'd never ruled. Dom pulled her close to his hard chest so she wouldn't fall to the cold marble floor, holding her tight but without cruelty. No doubt that would come later.

"Everything is going to be okay, Princess Eloise," he whispered against her ear. "I promise."

But it wouldn't. She knew better than to ever trust a man who promised happy endings in the middle of a kidnapping.

Chapter Two

Dominick Rasmussen tucked Princess Eloise closer against his chest as the elevator whisked them down to the subterranean garage and then opened its doors. He did a quick visual sweep of the space before stepping out, but it wasn't necessary. His team had been on surveillance duty for hours while he suffered through playing dress-up until a well-executed phone call sent Eloise's coworker on a wild goose chase to her child's school. Everything had gone perfectly, just as they'd planned…and that was the problem.

The kidnapping had been too easy, and it pissed him off. His anger beat against him in time with his footsteps, echoing against the concrete walls and parked cars in the nearly vacant space. The whole store had been a security nightmare. Getting up to the private personal shopping area required a special key card to open Dylan's main elevator on the eighth floor, but stealing one from the concierge on the main floor would have been child's play. Once on the showroom floor, there were surveillance cameras, but they were only angled to capture movement around the designer clothing, especially the pieces of couture displayed like artwork. There was a sideboard filled with snacks and drinks but no register to warrant another camera. That would be too uncouth for the überrich, who had their bills sent to their accountants, he supposed.

Then there was the employee-only area. Sneaking back there had taken the skill of a toddler on a mission to grab the last chocolate chip cookie. All he'd had to do was, literally, take a single step beyond a curtained wall. There weren't any surveillance cameras in the employee area, the elevator leading to the garage, or the roped-off parking area for eighth-floor shoppers. There wasn't even a damn valet waiting, because anyone who shopped on that exclusive floor had their own driver.

If the Fjende had gotten to her first, she'd be dead and his country would be lost forever. By staying away from her so long, he'd nearly guaranteed the violent coup that had allowed the Fjende to steal the throne would go unanswered. The Resistance would have sacrificed so much for nothing. Dom would do whatever it took to make sure that never happened. The royals would return to Elskov and retake the throne.

Princess Eloise sighed in his arms, her soft breath tickling the sensitive skin along his neck and sending a shot of lust straight to his cock. Without thinking, he tightened his hold on her. It was the wrong choice. She was small, only five feet, six inches, according to her file, but her curves filled his hands, pressed against his chest, and imprinted on his mind.

The flirting earlier hadn't been necessary for his mission, but he hadn't been able to stop himself. The Elle Olsen he'd met upstairs was a woman who needed to be flirted with, fucked hard, and satisfied completely. For a few minutes, he'd let himself believe he was the man for the job. Thank God he'd come to his senses and remembered she was pretending to be someone else just as much as he was. He could flirt with the shopgirl; he couldn't even make eye contact with the princess without her prior approval.

Pulling himself back from the brink again, he punched the button on his key fob and unlocked the Mercedes. She stirred in his arms and clutched the lapels of his suit as he lowered her into the passenger seat. The weakened chloroform he'd soaked the handkerchief in only needed to keep her knocked out until they made it to his secure compound in the mountains a few hours outside Harbor City, but already she struggled against it. Good. Elskov needed a strong ruler who'd fight, because the Fjende weren't going to give up power willingly.

He clicked her seat belt closed and shut her door before circling the silver coupe and getting in on the driver's side. The motor purred to life, and he pulled out of the garage, waving to the parking attendant as he did, making sure his raised arm and partially turned body blocked the man's view of the passed-out woman in the passenger seat. After merging into traffic, he pressed the button on the comm unit hidden in his tie clip. "The package is secure. See you at rendezvous point."

His cell rang exactly sixteen minutes later. The caller ID read "unknown number." Of course, he didn't need a name to know who was on the other end. He was surprised the Resistance's leader had waited this long. Dom put in his Bluetooth synced to the coupe; if the princess woke up on the drive, there would be trouble enough without her hearing the voice on the other end of this call. He hit the answer-call button on his steering wheel. "Good afternoon, sir."

"Is she okay?" the other man asked in his signature wheezy half croak, which was all that was left of his voice after the assassination attempt.

"Yes, everything went as planned." This operation had been in the works for a year, slow and steady to make sure the

Fjende weren't alerted to the princess's whereabouts. They'd planned so far ahead that they'd hacked into Dylan's internal server six months ago and put in a two-week vacation request for one Elle Olsen so her disappearance wouldn't cause concern. The timing for this had to be perfect.

"Did you have to get physical?" the other man asked.

Dom tightened his grip on the steering wheel. As if he'd hit a woman, let alone the one about to wear Elskov's royal crown. "No, sir. The chloroform eased the process."

"You better not have given her too much, dammit. Everything rides on her."

"I'm well aware of that." He reached across to her and pressed his fingers to the pulse point in her throat. Electricity singed his skin where he touched the smooth column of her neck, making his lungs tighten and his cock thicken against his thigh, but he held on long enough to confirm what he already knew. "Her breathing is steady and her heartbeat strong. She might have a headache when she wakes, but that should be it."

"Does she have an inkling about what's at stake?"

"We didn't get into that with her yet, sir." No, instead he couldn't stop flirting with her to see the light pink blush that climbed its way up from the sliver of cleavage visible above the scoop neck of the white sweater that clung to her, outlining every delicious curve. "I thought it would be prudent to get her out of Harbor City and have that conversation in a more private and secure location."

"Don't tell me where. The fewer specifics I know, the better. I thought we could risk a face-to-face prior to the Kronig, but that can't happen now. The Fjende are getting too close."

That was all it took to get his mind zeroed back in on what mattered. "Any sign that they discovered her location?"

"Nothing our spies have reported. Make sure it stays that way."

"It will," Dom said without hesitation.

"Don't get cocky with me. You lose focus, and everything goes straight to hell. We have one shot at this. You have a week to get her prepped and ready. No fuckups, Rasmussen." Per usual, the Resistance's leader hung up without a good-bye.

Dom clicked off the Bluetooth and pressed the gas pedal harder. After the violent havoc they'd caused in the coup during which most of the royal family had been killed, the Fjende had become the power behind the throne in Elskov. For ten years they'd plotted and planned, but with the Kronig coronation celebration in seven days, victory was within the Resistance's grasp, and he'd do whatever it took to make sure nothing interfered with the big day. The sooner he got the princess to his well-guarded compound, the better.

A couple of hours later, he passed through the gate guarded by two well-armed Resistance members and turned onto the half-mile drive. The entire twenty-acre compound covered the top third of Mount Livingston. The defensive position provided a perfect way to guard against intrusion. Motion sensors, surveillance cameras mounted at strategic locations, and enough armed muscle to take out a small army protected the rest of the property. He parked the car in front of the log château that had once been a vacation home for the Du Ponts. With fifteen bedrooms, servants' quarters, and a bunkhouse, it had acted as the Resistance's headquarters for the past ten years, but they'd be abandoning it soon, all thanks to the slip of a woman sleeping peacefully in the passenger seat.

Her skirt had worked its way up during the drive, showing off miles of long, muscular legs that made his mouth dry. He shouldn't look — she was his sovereign — but he was a man, one who'd dedicated his adult life to her whether she'd known it or not. Unable to resist, he looked. His gaze traveled over her tight body from her killer legs to the thin strip of creamy flesh at her narrow waist exposed by how her sweater had climbed up her body, to her full lips partially open in a relaxed O that made him wonder what they'd look like wrapped around his dick.

Fuck, he hadn't been this hard from looking since he'd been a teenager. He shook his head and forced himself to turn away. There was too much at stake to get lost between a pair of smooth legs, even if the stems in question didn't belong to the woman destined to rule his country.

He turned off the engine and exited the vehicle. No one appeared, but they'd been ordered to keep their distance and only approach if necessary. Spooking the princess any more than she probably already had been was not on the agenda. He rounded the car and opened the passenger door; she didn't move, and her breathing didn't change. Doubt tickled the back of his neck. He'd doused the handkerchief himself; the chloroform should be working its way out of her system by now. If she wasn't awake in the next half hour, he'd have to call in the medic on staff to help.

Scooping her up, he tried to ignore the way her head fit perfectly against his shoulder and how even in sleep she curled an arm across his chest as he strode across toward the château's front door. The slight hitch in her breath was his only warning. She snagged the nine-millimeter from his shoulder holster and pushed out of his arms in one fluid move before planting her feet shoulder width apart, holding the Glock in a comfortable grip that spoke of a woman who knew her firearms, and then aiming at his head.

"Put the keys in the ignition and then drop to the ground, face pressed to the driveway." A strand of reddish-blond hair flopped down onto her forehead, dipping down toward one brown eye. Without taking her steady gaze off him, she let out a hard huff of air and blew it out of the way. "Don't move after that and I won't have to kill you."

He brushed his fingertips across his tie, activating the comm unit. "Stand down and stay back." Then he took one step closer, putting the gun within reach of his long arms. "No offense, Your Highness, but that's not how things will be going down."

If she was surprised at him using her title, it didn't show.

She pushed the Glock's safety down with a smooth stroke of her thumb and slid back the top of the barrel to load a bullet in the chamber. "So you know who I am."

"I know everything about you." Right down to the fact that she slept in a ratty Fashion Institute of Harbor City T-shirt and wool socks pulled up to her knees.

One side of her mouth kicked up, curling her pouty pink lips into a smirk. "I doubt that."

He lunged for her right as she pulled the trigger.

Chapter Three

Elle knew guns like she knew the contents of her shoe closet. When it came to survival, she didn't mess around, but she hadn't planned for Dom. How could she? For such a big guy, he moved fast. In the half a heartbeat between tugging the trigger tight and the bullet clearing the chamber, he grabbed her wrist, wrapping his strong fingers around her tightly. Despite the adrenaline giving her an extra boost of strength, he managed to shove her arm up. The shot went wild.

He spun her around, slung his free arm around her waist, and yanked her to him. Her ass hit his iron-hard thighs. Fuck, those things were tree trunks in suit pants. The side of her head slammed against the unrelenting muscular slab of his chest. He kept her gun pointing at the cloudless sky.

Every nerve in her body was on high alert and tuned in to him—the steady *thump-thump* of his heartbeat against her cheek, the confidence in his stance as he wrapped himself around her as if he was protecting her instead of kidnapping her, the warmth of his body despite the fast-dropping temperature as the winter sun set early. He was bigger, stronger, and had already gotten the drop on her twice.

Third time's the charm. Get ready.

"I'm not the enemy." His hold loose but tight at the same time, Dom exerted only enough strength to keep her anchored to him and the gun pointed away from them both.

Dammit, she didn't want to believe him, but her survival instinct honed by ten years of hiding in plain sight told her she could. If he was with the people who had decimated her family, he could have killed her a thousand times over. He might not be the enemy, but that didn't mean she trusted him. She'd learned two important lessons when her father was murdered in that bloody coup: one, never trust anyone, and two, running was the key to survival.

"I'm with the Resistance." He curled his pointer finger and thumb together and straightened his middle, ring, and pinkie fingers in the Elskov royal guard's secret signal. "I'm here to help."

The Resistance. Made up of a mix of Elskovians and others, they'd sworn to never stop fighting to restore the monarchy and were rumored to have unlimited funds. Well, if a billionaire like Dom was behind them, that would explain their lack of money problems. Still, the instinct to run was stronger than her loyalty to a country that had killed her father. She twisted and squirmed against him, which accomplished nothing other than rubbing her sensitive breasts across his sinewy forearm. "Help who?"

"You."

The strain in his voice could have been from her escape attempts, but she doubted it. The bastard wasn't even breathing hard. Time to switch tactics. Instead of sinking her nails into the steel band he disguised as an arm, she inhaled a deep breath. As her lungs expanded, her boobs pressed against his forearm. He went perfectly still. Interesting. Now this was something she could work with. He could overpower her in a heartbeat, so she had to use whatever tools were at her disposal to distract, disarm, and defend. If Mr. Hard Body got a hard-on, that could very well be her ticket to freedom.

She lifted her chin, letting her left cheek rub against his hard pec as she tilted her face upward, and tugged at her bottom lip with her teeth as if she was a little slow and trying to work out all of the confusing details when in reality she was already ten moves ahead. "So while the world thinks of you as a real-life Bruce Wayne with hundreds of millions in the bank and models draped across your arm, you're really Batman, aligned with the Resistance, and you kidnapped me for my own good?"

"Exactly," he said.

"Isn't that what an assassin would say in such circumstances?" She batted her eyelashes.

He narrowed his gaze, but his lips twitched as if he were fighting off a smile. Shit. That might have been a step too far. Sometimes dialing down the drama proved harder than expected, but it was too late to pivot from her course now. She needed a second or two to break free—after that she'd figure it out.

"If you were on my hit list," he said, his voice low and soft, "you'd have been dead before you even got to ask me my inseam."

Thirty-four. The number popped in her head faster than an appropriate response.

"And if by 'such circumstances' you mean totally under my control..." His fingers brushed her hip as he dipped his head lower so his lips almost brushed her ear. "If that was the case, then I can't say I'd really be looking for talk."

His words tickled her sensitive skin, heated her flesh, and made her mouth go dry. Then he shifted his stance and something hard, long, and thick brushed against her ass before moving away. She dropped her gaze and bit her lip for real this time. It was either that or moan in protest. The man had a smart mouth, a hard body, and questionable motives. In short, he was exactly what made her panties melt.

"Are you sure you really want to play this game with me?" Dom asked, his lips so close to her ear she could practically feel them. "I promise, I'm much better at it than you."

She couldn't blame the frost in the air for the state of her nipples or the liquid heat curling in her belly. Dammit, this was not the time for her body to go all gooey and pliant. Or was it?

She let herself go slack. The two seconds when shock made him loosen his hold were her opening. She slipped underneath his arm and bolted forward. She had to get a few steps ahead of Dom's extralong wingspan, pivot and fire while on the run. *One. Two.*

Something—or, more exactly, someone—grabbed her by the hair and jerked her back. Pain shot through her, and she lost focus for a heartbeat. It was all the time Dom needed. He grabbed her gun arm and swung her around until the Mercedes was at her back and he blocked her in from the front. With an embarrassingly little amount of effort on his part, he twisted the Glock out of her fingers and flung it across the drive. Her scalp ached, but she wasn't about to give him the satisfaction of rubbing it.

"Going so soon?" he asked.

"The company isn't to my liking."

Dom raised one eyebrow, a smirk tugging up the edges of his full lips. Bastard. He knew. He knew she was pissed off, determined to escape, and so fucking turned on at the same time that just looking at him had her clenching her thighs together. It was official—she'd finally cracked. Ten years on the run, and her brain picked this moment to break. He crossed his arms, the move accentuating his thick biceps straining against his suit jacket. *Sweet mama.*

He glowered down at her. "Let's get one thing straight. You're not going anywhere without me. It's not safe."

"And you're safe?" He radiated danger the way her stove emitted heat.

"Without a doubt."

He wasn't here to hurt her, she believed him there. The Resistance were the good guys. They had been instrumental in getting her out of the country when the Fjende took power in the coup, but after they got her on the plane to America, she'd been on her own. Why had they come for her now? What had changed? "Who are you?"

"Dominick Rasmussen, international financier and playboy." He smiled, but there wasn't any joy in it. "I spend most of my time in London but have homes in Harbor City, Los Angeles, Sydney, and Madrid."

"No, who are you really?" Was he the Resistance's leader?

"Batman, remember?"

Frustration spilled over. This was her life, not a war game. The men behind the coup had killed her father and had their sights set on her, the next in line, when her father's aide had thrown himself in front of her, saving her life. She wouldn't dishonor their memory by just following along like a sheep. "If you can't give me answers, I'm not staying."

She'd find a way to survive on her own. She always had.

"You're staying," he said. "You don't have a choice."

"I always have choices." Sure, they were usually shitty, but after what had happened to her father, she made sure of it.

"Not in this case. This is bigger than you or me. Let's go inside. I'll tell you everything."

The temptation to follow his lead nearly overpowered her, but once she walked inside the massive château, she'd lose her best chance to escape, and escape had always meant survival. Her gaze flickered down at the Mercedes.

He took a step closer, angling his body so she'd have to

go through him to get to the door handle. "Don't even think about it."

"Can't blame a girl for having thoughts."

Dom's eyes darkened, and his gaze dropped to her lips. "Depends on what kind of thoughts."

And there it was, that zing of attraction that put her at the corner of insanity and desire. The man radiated confidence, strength, power, and even in these circumstances he made her body purr with want. If she couldn't ditch him, at least not yet, why not a little mental excursion that ended in Orgasmville? It was, after all, her favorite escape.

She closed the gap between them. "Why don't you show me what you're thinking?"

The vein in his temple throbbed, and he gulped. "That's not a good idea."

"Then stop thinking."

She did for the both of them. Acting on instinct and the need to find a little distance from the crazy turn her life had just taken, she lifted herself up onto her toes and kissed him.

It started out soft, an easy touch meant to tease as she parted her lips and sucked his bottom lip into her mouth, letting her teeth graze the tender flesh. He tasted of dark coffee, expensive chocolate, and knee-knocking, naughty talents that took her breath away.

The next thing she knew, his tongue was tangling with hers and his fingers were wrapped around her hair, pulling it taut and forcing her head at a better angle for him to devour her. It was hard. It was intense. It was a preview of how this man would be in bed, and she couldn't wait for that to happen. She squeezed her hand between their bodies and cupped his hard cock.

Dom let loose with a half groan, half growl before grabbing her by the hips and pushing against her from the front. He released her hair and snagged her wrists and held them out to the side, her palms pressed against the Mercedes, so she couldn't touch him as he rocked against her.

It was good—fuck that, it was amazing—but not enough. She needed more. She needed to feel him against her core. What she wouldn't give to wrap her legs around his lean hips. Whoever had invented the pencil skirt should be shot. She broke the kiss and grabbed him by the tie. "We need to get inside and lose the clothes unless you want to strip me naked and fuck me against your car. Either way, decide now."

A tiny, high-pitched squeal, almost like feedback, emitted from the silver clip on his tie. Dom froze against her before quickstepping it several steps away. He waved his hand over the tie clip, and the noise stopped. They stared at each other, both panting.

"What the hell is on your tie pin, Dom?" Anger and confusion mixed with regret and frustration inside her, twisting her gut and sucking out the last of the oxygen from her lungs.

Everything about him was hard and tense as he fisted his hands at his side. Lust made his blue eyes hazy, and for the first time since they'd met, he was breathing heavily.

He flicked his gaze from her to the driveway and to the sky before bringing it back to her…but not her eyes. His attention stayed firm on a spot below her eyes, and then he bent at the waist in a deep bow.

"Your Royal Highness, Princess Eloise, please accept my most sincere apologies for my most inappropriate behavior." Gone was the cocky billionaire, replaced with a more formal man of the royal court she remembered from before the coup. He straightened, but he didn't meet her eyes. "I'm the Resistance's second in command. We've been watching you since after you arrived in Harbor City ten years ago. We were hoping to never disturb you, as was your father's final wish. However, we have solid intelligence that the Fjende, who led the coup on your country, are coming for you." His icy, determined gaze met hers. "They mean to marry you off to your cousin Alton before killing you as soon as you produce an heir, but you shouldn't worry. We're going to stop them and take back Elskov."

Chapter Four

Everything after Dom's announcement was a blur. A numbness, the same that had trapped her for her first year in America, weighed down her limbs and clouded her brain. It was one thing to know—it was another thing to hear the words she'd feared spoken out loud.

They mean to kill you. The words were stuck on repeat in her head as he ushered her into the huge log cabin–style château and past the butler who looked like he could bench-press a Humvee. The incongruity of the MMA-fighter body tucked inside a formal black suit and white gloves, the same style the servants wore in Elskov Castle, jarred something inside her and revved up her survival-at-any-cost motor to burning-rubber speed.

"We need to talk." She used the imperial at-court voice her father had always affected when someone had displeased him greatly. "Immediately."

Dom didn't ask why. He didn't stop in confusion. He took her by the elbow and made a sharp right turn through the first available door. It was the kitchen. Once inside he dropped his hand and stole away the one bit of warmth from her while cold panic tried to break free. Needing time to get it under control, she clasped her hands together and inspected her surroundings.

The space was rustic meets modern. At one end of the large kitchen, a grouping of overstuffed chairs and a leather love seat in shocking hot pink sat facing a stone fireplace that took up half the wall. There was a spit in the hearth big enough to roast a medium-size pig. At the other end of the room, a gourmet stainless steel oven was nestled inside a stone wall, as were the oven's matching appliances. Everything was high-end, beautiful, and utterly impersonal. It was like looking at a magazine spread of what a chichi cabin in the woods should look like. If the coup had never happened, she probably would vacation in a château like this, with servants who doubled as security guards and sycophants who pretended to be her friends. She might not have friends now, but at least the few work friend–type relationships she had were on her terms and they were genuine. The last thing she needed was to go back to her old life, even if she could. There was nothing for her in Elskov besides memories of her father bleeding out on the palace steps and the realization that any sense of security was an illusion.

Her gaze landed on Dom, and a frisson of attraction sizzled across her skin. The bastard had kidnapped her, and she couldn't sever that vibrating line of want connecting them. The kiss outside had been a mistake. Dom wasn't like the men she took home after a night out. There was something harder, more dangerous about him. She could see it now when she looked beyond the generically Nordic features of cold blue eyes, light blond hair, and imposing size, a holdout from their Viking ancestors. Even in a mountain hideaway that was no doubt guarded like a fortress, and facing a woman he'd called princess and bowed down to outside, he couldn't hide the aggressive stance that was as much a part of him as it was of all the people in Elskov. Their home was a tiny island situated strategically between Norway and Scotland that had repelled invaders for centuries. The Elskovians never learned to fight. They learned to win, whatever the personal cost.

That's exactly what she'd do, but her final prize wasn't the crown of a country she hated—it was her own freedom. But first she had to survive, and to do that she needed Dom, at least for the time being.

"Tell me about the Fjende," she demanded as she circled the oversize granite island.

Dom arched an eyebrow, not missing the barrier she put between them. Then his gaze shot to the side, as if he'd remembered who he was and even more, who she was.

"They're a secret society behind the coup." He reached for a crystal decanter on the sofa table behind the love seat and poured two small glasses of champagne-yellow liquid. "Their reach is legendary. They orchestrated the attack on your father and then managed to convince the world that your father had a heart attack and died peacefully in his sleep, and that you agreed to let your cousin Alton act as your designee while in mourning."

"It's been ten years," she said. "How have they managed that?"

He strode across the room, the two glasses fitting easily in one of his large hands, and held them out to her. She took one and lifted it to her nose. The sweet and spicy, slightly peppery scent of caraway wafted up from the shot glass. Akvavit. She hadn't had the distinctly Elskovian spirit since the Christmas before her father died. He'd given her a sip of his, and it had burned its way down her throat like liquid fire, and he'd congratulated her on being strong enough to take it, just like he knew she always would be. The memory made her throat tighten with emotion.

"You don't keep up on the news at all." Dom shook his head and sipped his akvavit, not even flinching as he swallowed.

"I have my reasons." Like the fact that she hated her small island homeland, from its sheep farms to its rocky fjords. A man in a black raincoat might have shot her father, but she blamed the whole country for letting it happen, for not fighting back, for not seeing through the lies, and for abandoning her on a foreign shore.

Unlike the way she'd been taught, she shot back the akvavit in one gulp. It scorched her throat and made her eyes water, but she refused to react to the pain by gasping or wincing. She would remain impervious to it, as she was to all things Elskov. Once she was sure her hands wouldn't shake, she turned the shot glass upside down and placed it on the island.

Dom lifted his still mostly full glass in toast and took another small sip. "They had a princess impersonator. A few well-timed appearances over the years have kept the questions to whispers."

Good for them, the bastards.

"So why come after me at all? Surely they've realized by now that I have no interest in ever being Princess Eloise again." For all she cared, the island could sink to the bottom of the Atlantic Ocean.

"Because the Kronig coronation celebrating your official acceptance of your royal duties is less than a week away, and two days ago your impersonator died from an overdose."

Karma's a real bitch that way. Rounding the island, she swiped her glass and then made her way to the decanter and poured herself another shot.

"So they bury her and the sniveling Alton takes over." Ugh. That man had always been slimy and duplicitous. The fact that he'd work with the people who'd killed his own wife didn't shock her in the least.

"That's not how the line of succession works." Annoyance crept into his tone; it gave his already deep voice an inflexible cord that wrapped around her. "How do you not know this?"

The steel thread in his voice snapped her control in half.

"Because my father was forty-seven when the bastards murdered him, and it wasn't something I thought I'd have to think about for a long fucking time." She tossed back the akvavit like it really was the water of life its name translated to.

She welcomed the alcohol blaze as it slid down her throat and settled in her belly. It dulled the memories fighting to the surface—the wet, gurgling sounds her father made as he fought for breath, the dark burgundy of the blood gushing from his stomach. The way she didn't even fight the hand wrapped around her wrist, the one that stopped her from running to his side to comfort him in his last moments. She blamed Elskov for her father's death, but the guilt for letting him die alone was all hers. The silence screamed in her ears, and she concentrated to feel the last tinges of heat from the strong alcohol.

"Your Royal Highness, please forgive me," Dom said, executing another deep bow. "I shouldn't have said what I did."

"I'm not Princess Eloise. It seems she died of a drug overdose." She flipped the shot glass over and set it next to the decanter. "I'm Elle Olsen."

He drained the last of his akvavit and placed his glass next to hers. "We both know that's not true."

"It doesn't matter, because America is my home now. You want to play your spy-versus-spy games with the Resistance? Be my guest, but I won't be part of it."

"Princess, you don't have a choice." There was that unforgiving tone again, the one that allowed no disagreement.

Looked like someone was about to be a very disappointed

Mr. Hard Body. She raised her chin and narrowed her eyes at him. "I told you before, I always have a choice."

Dom closed his eyes and took in a deep breath. When he opened them again, he pinned her to the floor with a look of icy determination.

"Five days from now, the Kronig will take place," he said. "It can only take place with you in attendance. If you are not there to accept your royal duties, the crown must go to the next person in line for succession. That cannot be Alton, because he is married into the royal family. There is no one else, because the Fjende were thorough in their bloodletting. If you are not at the Kronig, the country will be thrown into chaos and the Fjende would not be guaranteed to have someone they control on the throne. They need you to take your place during the Kronig and marry you off to Alton so you can produce an heir that they can control."

That sounded perfectly unpleasant. "And after that, what is it? A shiv between the ribs?"

"For the past few years, they've let it be known that Princess Eloise is in precarious health—nothing specific, just enough to cover up the impersonator's increasingly limited appearances. Our theory is that they'll kill you and blame your long-standing but never named illness."

The bastards were thorough. She considered a third shot but knew that would knock her on her ass, and she needed to stay focused if she was going to figure out a way out of this shit storm she found herself in. And how exactly had she become embroiled in this? She'd been more than careful. She'd dyed her white-blond hair to the same strawberry blond as her favorite fictional teenage detective. Gone were her dark blue eyes, thanks to brown-colored contacts. She never stood out. She never spoke up. She'd been discovered anyway.

"Why won't the Fjende get another impersonator?" That would make things so much easier for everyone. They could have their little fiefdom, and she could go on living her quiet life of imposed solitude.

"The timeline is rather tight for that."

Frustration ballooned inside her, eliminating any space for fear or regrets or so-called royal duty. "So leave Elskov to find its own new leader."

"That would mean bloody civil war." He didn't yell. He didn't have to; the censure in his voice was enough. "There is no parliament, no legislative branch to take over if the monarchy dies suddenly. Thousands would die. Do you really want their blood on your hands because you didn't feel like doing your duty and wearing a crown?"

"That crown killed my father," she yelled in a harsh whisper to not draw undue attention. "That country let it happen. They deserve what they get."

"You can't mean that."

"Why, because it's my duty to sacrifice everything at the altar of Elskov?"

Blood beat against her eardrums, and heat pulsed in her cheeks as she glowered at Dom. How dare he try to drag her back into all this, back to the country that destroyed everyone she loved.

"No, because it's what your father expects. He bled for Elskov. Are you really willing to let his sacrifice be in vain?" This time Dom reached for the crystal decanter, poured a second shot, and downed it. "We need you to make a surprise appearance at the Kronig, because the Fjende can't make a move against you in public. A perfectly timed simultaneous surgical strike by the Resistance will destroy their leadership and cut off the head of the snake. Then you will take your rightful place on the throne."

"And then I become the Resistance's puppet?"

"No." He looked at her straight in the eye. "Then you become queen."

Queen. The role she'd been raised to assume. After her mother died, her father channeled his grief by telling his five-year-old daughter all about the great queens of Elskov. They'd been warriors, strategists, leaders—everything she was not. She was a stylist with a one-bedroom apartment in a sketchy neighborhood in Harbor City without close friends and who only had one-night stands because relationships were impossible when you were hiding who you really were. The realization of just how far she'd missed the mark her father had set blew through her like a hot wind down the main street of a ghost town, scattering emotional debris and leaving her empty and exhausted.

Dom reached out for her but stopped when his large hands were still inches away from touching her. He fisted his hands and brought them back to his sides. "All I'm asking for right now is that you don't say no."

Too weary to continue, she conceded this battle, knowing the war was far from over. "I have a feeling you wouldn't accept it anyway."

"Elskovians never surrender." He poured a third shot for each of them. The Russians and their vodka had nothing on the Elskovians and their akvavit. He handed her the glass, and their fingers brushed, and just like that the air around them again crackled with sexual tension. "They fight until they win."

"No matter the cost." On autopilot, she repeated the rest of the words emblazoned on the Elskovian state seal and tried to ignore her awareness of him.

He clicked his glass against hers in toast. "No matter the cost."

The alcohol barely singed this time as she sipped, watching him over the rim of her glass. She didn't know what this man was willing to sacrifice to get his way, but judging by the stony resolve reflected in his blue eyes, she imagined he'd give everything. It was both comforting and frightening.

Chapter Five

Night had turned the sky inky black hours ago, not that Dom had noticed. His eyes were glued to the woman shown on the small monitor in the mountain compound's security office.

He shouldn't be watching her. It was invasive. It was wrong. It was creepy. Yes to all of the above, but he kept his eyes glued to the monitor anyway, because he was an asshole. As long as he remembered that little fact, maybe he'd stop thinking about how five hours earlier he'd dry humped the future queen like a drunk college freshman behind the dorms. He would have done more—in fact, his balls still ached to do more—but the feedback from his comm device brought him back to reality lightning fast.

Ignoring the way blood rushed to his cock just from the memory of her pink lips and the way she'd felt pushed up against him, he focused on the bay of monitors in the security room.

There were surveillance cameras throughout the house's public areas. The monitor that had captured his attention showed the library tucked between Princess Eloise's bedroom and his. The door to the hallway remained shut, and to a newcomer that entry point seemed like the only way in. But there were secret doors to each of their bedrooms hidden behind bookshelves that were activated by hidden levers. On the bedroom side of things, the doors were hidden from the unobservant just as well, but she'd found hers. He couldn't help but admire her for that. The woman was more than a pretty face; her mind worked fast to connect the dots that left others wondering. If she hadn't already, she'd soon discover the small armory secreted behind a false wall in the back of her walk-in closet. He wouldn't expect any less from her. She hadn't made it through the past ten years on her own without any outside resources or support because she was an airheaded wimp.

He pressed a few buttons on the control pad, and the monitor showing the library went blank. "Let her have some privacy," Dom said. "It's been a rough day."

"Yes, sir," said Major Bendtsen as he sat in front of the console, never taking his eyes from the twenty monitors that played a rotating series of shots from strategic locations around the mountain compound.

"Status report."

"Everyone is on high alert but will remain as hidden as possible from view, as you ordered. Resistance One has been updated to her arrival. Our people in Harbor City and Elskov continue to monitor the Fjende operatives, but it doesn't seem they're aware the princess has been removed from her daily life."

"It won't stay that way for long, so don't lose focus." Not like he did every time he was near the woman. "Did you tell His Roy—" Dom stopped himself before he said the words that couldn't be spoken aloud, not even in this trusted space. "Did you tell Resistance One that she doesn't want to assume her duties?"

"No, sir."

He didn't blame the major. The messenger who delivered that news was bound to end up bearing the brunt of Resistance One's fury—or his own. Ten years' worth of strategizing to restore the monarchy to power and finally have his revenge on the Fjende who'd killed his family lay in the hands of a woman who didn't want anything to do with the plan. He had five days to persuade her to do her duty; if he didn't, the country went to shit, the Fjende would win, and his parents would remain unavenged.

That wasn't going to happen.

"Carry on." He slipped out of the security room, exiting through the door that from the other side looked like a working indoor waterfall.

The water feature at the end of the greenhouse had been set up so that the liquid was diverted any time the door opened from the inside and with the downward push on a garden gnome's red hat from the outside. He didn't know what kind of paranoid person had designed the château with its hidden passages and secret rooms, but it made it the perfect location for the Resistance's headquarters, and it had been his first purchase when he'd made his hundredth million eight years ago.

The air was hot and sticky inside the double-paned, bulletproof glass walls, and he slipped off his suit jacket as he crossed the clay-colored Spanish tile floor with its embedded sensors that detected changes in pressure—one of his little additions that added to the hidden appeal of the château. Emerging into the sitting room on the south end of the main building, he checked for the discreet surveillance hidden in the mounted taxidermy so cleverly—one of the stag's black eyes was a camera. It was the same with the heat-sensitive motion detectors in the oak-lined hallway, the weight-activated alarms on the stairs, and the concealed visual spying devices throughout the château. If he relaxed his guard here in the mountains, it was because it was the one place in the world he could.

He paused for a moment outside the library door to give himself enough time to suck in a deep breath and then entered the room.

"I was wondering where you'd run off to." She flicked on one of the Tiffany table lamps. The soft light created a dim halo around her body, outlining every delectable curve. "For a large house, there sure aren't a lot of people around." She paused and arched an eyebrow. "Or are there?"

So that's how they were going to play this, huh? The challenge in her voice did something to him. Made him want to push her right back, see how she reacted, and find out if he could get her to lose some of that cool control on display. *Let the games begin.*

"You know there are." He shut the door behind him and leaned against it, another nonverbal reminder that she might be royalty, but here in this château he was the one in charge.

"How many?" she asked, her tone light, but he wasn't fooled.

"Enough." No one knew *all* the specifics of security except for him, not even Major Bendtsen, who acted as his second in command. Some would call it paranoia. He preferred to think of it as the ultimate safety measure.

She sauntered over to the bookshelves and let her slim fingers slide across the books' spines as she made her way to the hidden door that led to her bedroom. Stopping at just the right spot, she pulled out a first edition of *Huck Finn*. The shelf swung open on silent hinges, revealing her room.

"And the *Scooby-Doo* haunted house doors?" she asked.

He would not look at the king-size bed visible through the opening. Imagining her naked on that bed was the last thing his big or little head needed at the moment. "They came with the house, Your Royal—"

She held up a hand. "Elle." Her voice was hard, imperial. "That's who I am now."

So stubborn.

"As you command...Elle." The name tasted sweet on his tongue, like a secret dipped in honey.

"What happens if I walk out the front door?"

As if he'd let that happen. "The Fjende will find you and, eventually, kill you."

Pondering this bit of information, she twisted a long strand of silky reddish hair around her finger as she stared at him. It was as if she could see something inside him that he didn't know was there. The idea was touchy-feely, weird, and completely unshakable. He didn't like it one bit.

Elle crossed over to him, stopping well out of arm's reach before walking a half circle around him and putting him on the spot. She inspected him from top to bottom, her gaze lingering for a couple of beats on his pants, where his cock lay against his thigh. Blood rushed to it in response, but he refused to move or adjust his stance. She knew what she did to him. She'd felt it as he'd slid against her firm, high ass outside, a moment of blissful agony he'd no doubt jerk off to soon. But he knew the score. She was trying to exert control over the situation by making him hard with just a look. Well, she wasn't going to get it. Control was his. Always.

With deliberate care, she scraped her teeth across her plump bottom lip, sending a shot of hunger through him that took his breath away. "What happens if I stay?"

"I'll keep you safe." He would. No matter the cost.

"Why?" she asked, a huskiness invading her tone.

"It's what I do." It's how he'd get his revenge. Finally.

She stepped closer, her breath warm against his ear. "Who are you?"

"Dominick Rasmussen." The lie came out smooth and

soft, despite the way his body had hardened because of her nearness and the line of questioning.

"Bullshit." Her laugh teased his skin, and then she was gone, striding across the library to her phone lying on the seat of an oversize leather chair. She bent over, giving him a heart attack–inducing view of her ass encased in that tight green skirt of hers, and picked up her phone. Turning, she scrolled through whatever was on the tiny screen. "I still get cell coverage up here in the snowy boonies of these mountains. Eight years ago you appeared out of nowhere, one of the wealthiest men in the Western Hemisphere, with a mysterious past and a never-ending supply of cash."

"Everyone comes from somewhere." For him it was a place he'd never see again because it no longer existed, not the way he remembered. Pain pinched his lungs as the memories flooded. The blood. The severed limbs. The blank stares of the dead.

She flung her cell back onto the chair. "Tell me."

This needed to stop—the questioning, the wanting, the hunger that nearly dropped him to his knees. Stalking across the sixteenth-century Turkish rug, he trapped her between himself and the chair. "It has no bearing on today or what we're going to accomplish in the days ahead."

He let his frustration boil close enough to the top that she should have wilted in the heat. She didn't. He was beginning to realize that she burned just as hot as he did. Underneath the expensive clothes and their arctic Elskovian exteriors, a blue flame flickered in them both. If he wasn't careful, that heat might end up turning a decades-long dream to ash.

Her gaze grew hooded, and a pink flush ate its way up her ample cleavage, but her questioning continued. "You live in London, but you don't have an English accent. Instead, you have the slightest hint of Brooklyn and something that"—she narrowed her eyes—"sounds a lot like home."

"I thought you were a woman without a country."

"I am," she whispered.

The loneliness in her voice tore a hole through him. The Resistance had watched, but always from a distance. What kind of life had that been for her? He'd spent the last ten years surrounded by fighters readying for battle. She'd lived those years alone; it was all there in her file on his hard drive.

She lifted her small hand to his chest, setting it over his fast-beating heart and sending shock waves through him. With the barest pressure, she pushed him back as far as her arm would go. He allowed it even though every instinct in him was screaming for him to wrap her up and tell her she would never be alone again.

"What will it take to convince you you're wrong, that you have a country, a home?"

The lost look in her brown eyes gave way to a wary determination. "A good place to start would be the truth."

Now, that way lay trouble. "About what?"

"You." She brushed past him, putting half of the rug between them, as if that would minimize the awareness he had for her. "According to the internet, you're a total player with the Midas touch when it comes to business deals. According to you, your only mission in life is to get my ass on the Elskov throne. So which is it?"

They stared at each other as the silence stretched between them, holding them in place. Talking about his past had been forbidden for so long, he wasn't sure he could speak the words out loud. He took a deep breath, the smell of tear gas and the echoes of horrified screams escaping from some dark place in his memory. She didn't know. How could she? The Fjende had covered their tracks too well. The international community had accepted the state-sanctioned stories of the king's sudden heart attack and a grieving nation temporarily broken apart by rival factions as an explanation for the riots, the murders, and the chaos following the coup.

Telling her everything wasn't an option. Success depended on her never finding out the truth about her father, but the rest? That he could give her.

"Do you remember what the week leading up to the coup was like?" He shoved his fingers through his hair as if he could wipe the memory from his brain. "I was twenty-two and home on holiday from university. I thought I was about to take over the world—then everything crumbled."

The reports in the beginning had been sporadic rumors, but they could only be contained for so long. Elskov was a small country, and on their island word traveled fast.

The heated pink in Elle's cheeks drained until only a ashy pallor was left. She clutched her hands together in front of her. "My father tried to hide it from me as long as possible, but everything was so tense there really wasn't any way. There were paid protestors outside the castle gate. Someone had to taste my food before I could eat it. In the last few days, I wasn't allowed to leave the castle, even in the armored SUV."

In those last few days, the country was obsessed with sightings of royalty, false or not. "The Fjende claimed your lack of visibility was proof your family had abandoned the country."

"My father would never have done that." She shook with indignation as disgust wound its way into words. "He bled for Elskov, for all the good it did. The coup won anyway."

Her words slapped him in the face, and he nearly flinched. "The war isn't over yet."

"What war?" She spun around to face him, her eyes blazing with fury. "No one in the international community cares about Elskov. They gladly eat up the bullshit that I'm alive and sorta well, that no coup ever took place, and that my father died of a heart attack and everything is business as usual."

"We can change that." The frustration of being so close to what he'd worked so hard for and discovering there was yet another hurdle to climb ripped a hole into him. Moving forward could be done without her cooperation. He'd committed to doing what needed to be done, no matter the cost. "*You* can change that."

She opened her mouth, but nothing came out. Instead, she let out a deep sigh, closed her eyes, and the fight went out of her. For a moment she stood there, her shoulders slumped, before opening her eyes and hitting him with a question he'd skated around answering for years. "You don't need this. Why do you want it so fucking badly?"

"You're wrong. I do need this. I've been waiting for ten years to make it happen." The words came out before he could stop them, even if he'd wanted to. "You're right on the accent. I had the best language and dialect tutors, but they weren't good enough for someone with your ears. I grew up in Elskov as a registered foreigner. My family was wealthy but still waiting to become official citizens. Despite that, my parents were loyal royalists. They were not quiet about their support of your father and pledged to do whatever it took to help him. The wrong people heard about this and decided to make an example of them." He fisted his hands, pushing past the agony the words brought to the forefront. "The night your father was shot and you fled for America, they were murdered. Their mutilated bodies were displayed in the square near Elskov Castle to serve as a warning to other loyalists. It worked."

He didn't know when she'd walked over to him, but suddenly she was there standing in front of him and taking his large hands into her own small ones. "I'm so sorry."

Stopping the story there was the smart thing. It allowed him to hold a little bit of the pain back, but he needed to tell her. He had to let her know that although she might have been alone, she hadn't been abandoned.

"Their names were Sabine and Rasmus Vinter," he said, his parents' names so long unspoken that they seemed foreign on his tongue.

She gasped and released him as if he'd burned her.

"Yes, the same Sabine and Rasmus who were supposed to meet you in Harbor City and keep you safe after you'd escaped," he said. "It took me a year and you don't want to know how many bribes to track you down. You'd hidden yourself well."

"I didn't have a choice."

"But you do now." He took her hands in his. They disappeared in his grasp, reminding him that behind the larger-than-life image of her he'd created, she was in many ways the lonely stylist working a nine to five, surrounded by luxurious trappings that probably only reminded her of how her former life had ended in tragedy. "You said yourself that you always have a choice. I'm asking you to make the right one."

• • •

Elle looked down at their hands. She was trapped. Not by him, but by his expectations and his agenda. If she said yes, that would be her life until she ended up alone, like her father, her blood soaking the ground of the country he'd loved that had betrayed him, because that's how it would end. The Fjende wouldn't give up power without a fight, and she was no one's idea of a warrior queen. She was just Elle. She'd fail, and what would that do to her father's legacy?

Hating that it was so hard to do, she pulled her hands from his. "No."

Dom snapped to attention, an icy contempt freezing out the emotion she'd seen in the blue depths of his eyes only moments before. "What do you mean, no?"

"I'm Elle Olsen." She wiped her palms against her pencil skirt, trying to numb the electric tingling touching him created. "I'm a stylist. I live in a tiny one-bedroom, rent-controlled apartment in Harbor City. Find another way. I can't be your queen."

"That's bullshit." Anger roughened the low timbre of his voice until it was like sandpaper against her last thin string of control. "It's time to stop hiding who you really are."

"Fine advice coming from you." And there it went. The string tethering her to a place of calmness snapped in half, and her temper erupted, heating up her insides and melting the bone-chilling, furious fear holding her in place. "You haven't been hiding at all, have you, with your fake last name and all-too-convenient information blackout on all things related to your Elskov history?"

"This isn't about me," he said through gritted teeth. "This is about you taking your rightful place as queen. It's time you accepted your duty. You're being selfish."

"Selfish?" The smug bastard. As if she wouldn't be giving up her life—her freedom—as soon as she put on that crown, but she should just accept it like a good little girl. She hadn't been a good little girl since the night her father died. She couldn't bring him back, but she damn sure wouldn't help the country that destroyed him. "Elskov took everyone I loved and abandoned me in a foreign land."

"You were never alone," he said.

The statement was so demonstrably false that she laughed, *laughed*, right at that big, broad chest of his, but there was nothing joyous in her voice. Instead there was the hurt and fear and despair of a seventeen-year-old girl who, within a twenty-four-hour time span, had seen her father murdered, left the only home she'd ever known, and found herself alone on a bench outside the Harbor City International Airport, totally ill prepared to function in the real world outside the castle walls.

"Now who's full of shit? Were you there when I spent a month holed up in a cheap hotel because I was petrified that if I left someone would kill me?" She jabbed a finger hard into his unrelenting chest, the frisson of attraction mixing with the emotions swirling around inside her like a tornado no one could control. "Were you there when I realized no one was coming for me and that I had to create a new life for myself? Were you there when I was turned down for every job I applied for because the only thing I knew how to do was wave, smile, and put together a killer outfit?" She fought to get the words out through her tightened throat. "Were you there when I pawned my mother's gold locket, the last tie I had to her, so I could buy forged identification papers and actually create a new life for myself?" Biting the inside of her cheek to head off the tears threatening to spill, she straightened up to her full height. "No, you weren't. No one was."

Raw emotion squeezed her lungs as she stared at him. Large and imposing, he loomed over her, the cold fury of his anger and their potent sexual chemistry sucking up all the oxygen in the room. The air sizzled around them, sparking with too many wants denied. His icy-blue gaze dipped down to her mouth, and her stomach dropped down to her knees. He stepped closer, eliminating the space between them and sending her heart rate through the roof. He didn't touch her. He didn't have to for her to feel him. Something hot and angry sparked between them. He looked as if he couldn't decide whether to fight her or fuck her. She knew the feeling.

"You owe it to your country," he said, but his words burned with a different kind of heat than before, one that stoked an answering blaze within her.

"And it owes me my father back." The agony of those words had her running for an escape, the kind where she ended up naked, sweaty, and too satisfied to do anything but breathe, because thinking…remembering…feeling was killing her right now. "Is he going to magically rise from the dead when I put that crown on my head? He died for them, for Elskov."

"Do you really think he would have had it any other way?" Dom asked. "Do you really think he would have saved his own life if it meant sacrificing his country?"

No, he wouldn't, and that was the broken shard of glass that cut against her heart every time she thought of him. Her father had loved her. She'd never doubt that, but Elskov, his duty, the crown—they all came first. And in the end, the truth of it was that she and his beloved country had both abandoned him as he lay dying. The guilt surrounding that moment never went away, but sometimes she could outrun it by shutting off her brain and letting her body take over. That's exactly what she needed right now.

The tension between her and Dom had been winding her up since he'd walked out of the elevator and on to the Dylan's showroom floor. She needed release. He could give it to her. Giving in, she reached up with both hands and grabbed fistfuls of his button-up shirt as she raised herself to her tiptoes, bringing her mouth in line with his.

"We can't do this," he said, his words brushing against her sensitized skin, but even though he easily could have, he didn't break her hold on him. "You're my queen."

She stilled, millimeters from his full lips. "Not tonight."

"And tomorrow?" he asked, but his hands had already settled on her hips, yanking her closer so there was no missing exactly how hard he was for her.

"Stop talking." She nipped at his bottom lip as she tugged at his shirt, sending the buttons flying. "And fuck me."

Chapter Six

Dom took her mouth, answering her desperate plea disguised as a demand. It wasn't a dim lighting, romantic music, or flower petals kind of kiss. Neither of them wanted—needed—that right now. It was possession.

She was right. Tonight, she wasn't his queen. She was Elle Olsen, the woman he'd wanted to taste, touch, and fuck since he laid eyes on her in that sexy secretary outfit that hugged her hips and accentuated her bountiful tits. He'd flirted. She'd teased. He'd kidnapped her. She'd shot at him and tried to knee him in the balls. It wasn't exactly relationship starter material, but that wasn't a possibility for them anyway. No matter what it took, tomorrow he'd make sure she'd agree to be Elskov's sovereign, and he'd be her loyal subject, but tonight he was going to hear Elle scream out his name as she came.

Step one was to show her who was in control. He threaded his fingers through her long, silky hair and fisted it, pulling it tight and tilting her head back so he could deepen the kiss. He delved into her mouth, letting his tongue tease and tempt her until she moaned. That sound nearly sent him over the edge. His cock, so warm and thick against his thigh, throbbed. What he'd meant to do was drive her to the brink, and instead here he was ready to dive over into the abyss.

In an effort to take things back down to a slow, controlled burn, he traced a path across her jawline and down her neck with his lips, tasting the forbidden sweetness of her skin. But Elle wasn't having it. She popped open the few buttons left on his shirt and pushed a hand inside. His entire world shrank down to two points—her soft hand against his hard chest and her pulse beating like mad against his insatiable mouth. It would be so easy to get lost in her, and that couldn't happen.

He dragged himself away from her neck, giving the creamy column one last lick and nibble before circling around her. Her confusion was palpable as she pivoted, following his progress. Perfect. He wanted her off balance. He had the feeling it didn't happen often. Stopping at the side table, still within touching distance because he couldn't seem to make himself go any farther, he noticed a small button had landed next to the decanter. His tailor on Savile Row was going to be in a snit over the state of Dom's shirt. He picked up the button.

"Hold out your hand," he said, not sure who was more surprised when she immediately did. He put the small, pale, circular disk in the center of her palm and folded her hand closed. "I should make you pick up every one of those buttons before I let you come."

The corners of her mouth curved into a sensual smile, and she jutted out a hip. "Let me?"

"That's right." He traced a finger across the curve of her cashmere sweater, loving how she shivered under his touch, her stiff nipples tenting the soft material. "You want to fuck me—and we both know you do—then we do it my way."

Watching him through the screen of her thick lashes, she

tugged her bottom lip through her teeth. "You need to work on this whole control thing."

Yeah, that wasn't going to happen. Control wasn't the most important thing; it was everything. "You'll like my way. You're already wet thinking about it, aren't you?"

Her quick intake of breath was all he needed for confirmation. Resisting the urge to beat his chest like some sort of caveman, he poured himself a finger of honey-colored liquid and sat down in the leather club chair, folding his leg so his ankle rested on top of his knee. Each movement was precise, executed with deliberate slowness to draw out the moment, increase the tension between them until it was nearly unbearable. Elle rushed, and it was time she learned the pleasure of a leisurely pace. Taking a sip of akvavit, he wished he hadn't stopped smoking. A good cigar right now would give him something to do with his free hand that didn't involve touching her. It wasn't easy. Good thing he never liked anything simple; the harder the better the victory at the end.

"And what does your way entail?" she asked, looking down at him with a mix of curiosity and hunger.

Her husky voice was as good as a hand wrapped around his dick. The woman was fucking lethal to his self-control. Downing his drink and walking away was the smart move, the right move. He should get up right now, but there was no fucking way that was going to happen. As long as he stayed smart about things, he wouldn't lose control. He sat back in his chair as if he wasn't about to spontaneously combust. "I want to see what you've learned."

Her brown eyes widened in surprise. "Excuse me?"

"I know all about the time in Vegas. I forget, was the window that you were pressed naked against on the sixteenth floor?" His cock twitched beneath his pants. The brief mention in the surveillance report had him hard for days, no matter how many times he'd jacked off. "And then there was the time you came while sitting in that corner booth at the restaurant with your lover's fingers buried in your sweet pussy. My favorite, though, was the supply closet in the dance club." He sipped his drink, burning too hot to feel the liquid fire as it made its way down to his stomach. "You shut the door so I couldn't watch, but I stood guard outside and listened. I didn't know a person could make such a desperately blissful noise."

The sweetest pink flush made her bad girl curves rosy. "You were there?"

"That time?" The sound she'd made had embedded itself into his fantasies, but when he had stroked his cock, she wasn't moaning wordlessly—she was calling his name. "Yes."

Her hand on her hip and the downturn to her sensual lips all screamed displeasure, but the lusty gleam in her eyes was anything but censorious. "We're going to talk about this after."

"About how we watched you or about your lovers?"

She narrowed her eyes, and this time it wasn't just desire smoldering in her gaze. "Are you trying to shame me?"

"Fuck, no, especially not when I'm about to hear that sexy moan of yours while you're naked in front of me."

"Is that what you want?" she asked. "Me naked?"

"It's a start." He had a list, a long one that started with naked and ended with too tired to ever come again.

"So where should I begin?" She stepped between his splayed legs as she toyed with the hem of her sweater. "With this or…" She brought one stiletto-shod foot up so it rested on the seat in front of his groin, the toe of her shoe brushing ever so lightly against his balls. She bent forward and ran her hands up her legs, pushing up her skirt and revealing the lacy tops of a pair of thigh highs held up by black satin garters. She glided her fingertips over the snap holding them in place. "Or here?"

His mouth went dry, and his lungs pinched closed. "Leave

them on."

"Careful." She put her leg down and smoothed her skirt. "I was afraid you were going to pass out on me. You gotta remember to breathe."

Cheeky girl. She'd learn, and soon. "Sweater."

Elle didn't ask what he meant, didn't turn shy. She stripped the fuzzy white material off her, exposing a sheer nude bra that did nothing to disguise how hard her nipples were or how full and heavy her tits were. The sweater slipped to the floor, unneeded and unwanted.

"Skirt."

Gliding the backs of her fingers over her curves, she slid her hands lower and around the indent of her waist to the back of her skirt. Blood rushed south, leaving him light-headed but unable to look away as the material gaped and then skimmed over her round hips, down her long legs, and landed in a pool of green around her ankles.

If he didn't run five miles a day and spend at least an hour in the gym several times a week, he would have worried about keeling over as his brain short-circuited while viewing the goddess in front of him. She was Freya come to life—love, lust, beauty, sorcery, fertility, gold, war, and death were wrapped up into one breathtaking woman.

"Walk for me." The words sounded torn from his throat, raw and desperate.

She arched an eyebrow but turned and strutted away from him. Since he'd spent the day staring at her butt and never saw a panty line, he'd expected a thong. Instead, she wore a pair of sheer panties that stopped halfway across her ass, accentuating the high, round curve of her flesh. A black satin garter belt lay flat against her creamy skin, long lines of slim ebony ribbon making lines down the backs of her thighs to the thigh highs.

"That's far enough," he said when she'd made it to the

edge of the rug and spun around to face him. "Does my watching you make you wet?"

"I don't know that I can get any wetter." Her pink tongue darted out and flicked against her lips, leaving them slick and shiny.

Yep, that smart mouth of hers and sinful body were going to kill him before the night was out. "Does your pussy ache for me?"

She nodded, her brown eyes heavy lidded and full of promise.

Not good enough. He wouldn't let her run tonight, not from herself, not from him, and definitely not from the attraction burning them both from the inside out. "Say it."

She lifted her chin in a stubborn tilt and didn't make a sound.

"If you say it, I can make that ache all better. If you don't, I won't." A total lie. There was no way he wasn't tasting all of her tonight.

No doubt she knew exactly how big of a liar he was, but she played along by batting her eyelashes. "How are you going to make it better?" she asked, her voice as soft as her curves.

"I'm going to kiss it and make it better." He set down the tumbler. The akvavit had lost all flavor, because the only thing he wanted to taste was her. "Isn't that what you want, my lips on you? My tongue? My fingers stretching you until you aren't sure if you're feeling pain or pleasure, you just don't want it to stop?"

"Yes."

"Yes what?"

"My pussy aches for you to fill me up so I can ride you until I climax so hard my walls milk you dry."

He nearly came in his pants just from hearing the words rolling off her delicious, very un-princess-like tongue. "Get over here."

For a second she didn't move, not even a smart-ass twitch to her shiny pink lips. Blood pounded in his ears in its rush to his painfully hard cock. If she didn't get her sexy ass over here soon, he was going to implode. He dug his fingers into the chair's leather arms, an anchor in a blizzard of lust that had him blind to everything but her. Finally she moved just as he was on the precipice of breaking his own cardinal rule—relinquishing total control and giving in by being the first to move. Relief and anticipation whipped through him as he watched the show of a lifetime. Elle strutted toward him, her full hips swaying with every step, as she watched him with unblinking intensity, everything about her screaming a challenge at the same time as she gave in to his demands. His heart beat in time with each stomp of her skinny heels as she crossed the rug and stopped in front of him.

"Do you like these?" He slipped his finger beneath the edge of her panties, curling a finger around the middle and pulling it so the material bunched and nestled between her slick folds. Leaving it in place, he withdrew his finger without touching her any more, despite her mewling protest. He held up his finger, admiring how it glistened in the light. God, she was wet—he sucked the moisture from his finger—and sweet.

"I'd like them better off me."

"Really?" He leaned forward and swiped his tongue over her swollen bare lips. "I think they look pretty right where they are."

Her fingers dug into his scalp, tugging his face closer to heaven's door.

Normally, he would have pulled back at that, refused to cede control, but with Elle nothing seemed to go as expected. She not only surprised him, she made him surprise himself. Without hesitation, he buried his face between her shaking thighs, cupping her ass to tilt her hips and give him a better angle. Licking and lapping against her folds and the silk between them, he explored her—claimed her—with his tongue. Their wetness mingled, soaking the slip of material covering her entrance and adding an extra layer of friction that would take her higher, faster, which was exactly what he wanted, a quick explosion followed by a torturous, blissfully slow burn that would melt them both. He sneaked a finger under her damp panties, then another, and slid them home inside her warmth. Stroking and stretching her entrance, he plunged inside again and again, being sure to rub against her swollen and sensitive G-spot. The sounds she made, moans of ecstasy punctuated by unintelligible words in their native tongue, spurred him on until she encompassed the entirety of his world.

Pushing her center to him, she undulated against his mouth, using him with the desperate need of those on the edge of coming apart. "Dom," she screamed and rewarded him with the flood of her orgasm against his tongue.

Not giving her time to slide into satisfied oblivion, he swept her up and turned toward the hidden door to her room. She was so light in his arms, the perfect fit as she laid her head on his shoulder, her long, silky hair mussed and ticking his neck.

"Where are you taking me? I wasn't done with you yet." She sighed, and her eyelids drooped.

"Believe me, I'm far from through with you." Not by a long shot. He had one night, and he wasn't going to waste a moment. "We're going to the bedroom so I can spread you out on that giant bed and really take my time."

Her eyes snapped open. "No."

"Why?" He paused, his hand halfway to the copy of *Huck Finn* that would send the bookcase swinging open.

"That's my space." She pushed out of his arms, landing on her feet, and then backed up a few paces. "It makes all of this personal."

"It *is* personal." How could it not be, with her taste still on his tongue?

"No." She shook her head. "It's not. Sex never is."

Her words were like lightning hitting dry brush, setting off a wildfire of unexplainable anger through him. Happily ever afters weren't in the cards for people like him, whose lives were devoted to a cause greater than themselves, and especially not with a princess who was soon to be his queen. One-night stands were part of his repertoire, but they'd never been impersonal or anonymous. His stomach tightened. "Then you have no fucking clue about great sex."

"I never would have taken Mr. I Give the Orders as a romantic." Rolling her eyes, she snorted. "Look, we get each other off, we scratch an itch. None of it matters. It's just sex with better orgasms than if I was left to my own devices."

It shouldn't have mattered. He was a man with a hard dick and a willing, beautiful woman. The situation was one a million men would give their left nut to be in, but it pissed him off. "I've got no interest in being a breathing dildo for you to get off on."

"Too bad, because I don't do emotional connections." She jerked *Huck Finn* from the shelf, releasing the door. "Good night."

She hit the corresponding mechanism on the other side of the wall and closed the hidden door, shutting him out without even the briefest look back.

The princess was a bitch, and he was, no doubt, a total asshole. The whole situation was fucked, and he still had to persuade her to fight for her crown.

• • •

Elle held it together until the bookshelf swung closed before sinking to her knees, her whole body shaking and blackness threatening her vision. Forcing in a slow, deep breath, she closed her eyes and pictured a green field under a perfect blue sky. She exhaled, draining all of the air from her lungs and then inhaling through her nose until her chest expanded as far as it would go, the whole time hearing the sound of the salt-scented Elskovian breeze rushing up from the fjords and out over the long grass. That field north of the capital was her happy place, not the castle where she'd grown up, with its thick gray stone walls and ornate wrought-iron decorations. She'd played in it as a girl, the golden tufts atop the grass tickling her calves as she chased the fluffy white sheep that roamed there. Opening her eyes, she came back to the here and now. Another ragged in and out, and the black dots dancing on the edges of her vision faded away, her heart stopped trying to tear out of her chest, and the all-too-familiar panic sheathed its claws.

That had been a close one. Another minute with Dom and she would have let him into her bed, the first man to have ever been there. All of the others had been fast fucks in borrowed spaces followed by a quick good-bye. It was the best way to make sure they only saw the her she wanted them to see, not the woman she really was. Keeping it impersonal kept her safe, kept her alive, and kept her sane.

But Dom already knew who she was, so there was no danger of a stray word spoken in her sleep or a nightmare that curled around her throat, squeezing it tight, until she jackknifed awake, ready for battle with the dreamland ghosts she couldn't touch. For some reason that scared her more. She hadn't openly been herself for a decade and didn't know if she could. She'd been born a princess, but that didn't mean she knew how to be a queen.

She shivered, chilly in her underwear and silk thigh highs without Dom's face-of-the-sun heat nearby. Hoping for a T-shirt or sweats left behind from a previous guest, she opened the heavy, wood dresser drawer. She gasped. It was filled with her underwear. She pulled open another drawer... her shirts...another...her workout clothes. Leaving the dresser with its drawers open like they'd been ransacked, she sprinted across the plush carpet to the mirrored closet doors and flung them wide, only to find the walk-in closet filled with her own dresses hung according to color and shoes displayed by heel height, just like she did at home.

The bastards. They weren't going to let her leave until she said yes. Her feet sank into the plush cream carpet as she paced in a wide arc from the French doors leading out to a private balcony, around the sturdy walnut four-poster bed and across to the eggshell-white chaise lounge decorated with small silver faux fur pillows. That's where, earlier in the evening, she'd slept off the mixture of akvavit and whatever Dom had used to drug her prior to hauling her here.

Her options were limited. She knew where she was, thanks to Google Maps and the GPS in her phone. However, calling for help wasn't an option, because who the hell was she going to call? The cops? The story of the lost princess would be front-page news in Harbor City before she even finished giving her statement. The Fjende would have a sniper on her as she walked out of the police station. She could hit the road on her own, but she didn't have money or a car. Relying on the kindness of strangers had never worked out for her before, and she sure as shit didn't expect it to now. Stealing Dom's car wasn't an option. She'd seen the cameras peppered throughout the compound. Until she knew enough about the security layout to avoid them completely—or got the anonymous all-seeing eyes to trust her enough to look away occasionally—she didn't have a hope of getting near the compound's garage without company.

That's it.

She needed to get Dom to trust her. He'd said they had

almost a week before the Kronig. That gave her more than enough time to placate him, get him to believe she was on board with his crazy take-back-the-throne plan. She glanced back at the closed hidden door leading to the library. Too bad she'd royally fucked up the perfect opportunity to do just that.

Chapter Seven

Dom punched the blue mug button on the most important machine in his life at the moment. Nothing happened. In another ten seconds, his vision was going to turn as red as his bloodshot eyes after a night spent staring unblinkingly at his ceiling. The coffeepot had too many fucking buttons. What was wrong with a plain old ordinary coffeepot that didn't need little single-serve cups and eighty billion buttons?

"You need to add water," Elle said from behind him.

His muscles locked, and he tightened his grip on his coffee cup. That the mug managed not to break in his grasp was a testament to quality Elskovian manufacturing. *That voice.* He hadn't stopped hearing both her sweet moans and her subsequent dismissal in his head since she'd disappeared last night.

"Here, let me show Mr. Big Bucks how things work in the real world where people have to make their own coffee." She slid into the narrow space between him and the wall and removed the clear plastic container from the side of the infernal machine. The smell of fresh soap and flowery shampoo clung to her. "Excuse me."

Still not looking in her direction, he took a step back and gave her access to the sink. Short of closing his eyes like a dog shoving its head under a pillow to avoid something that was only going to get him into trouble, there wasn't a damn thing he could do to stop from seeing her as she stepped in front of him and turned on the water before grabbing a mug from the open cabinet. Her long hair spilled down her back in wavy, still damp strands. Unable to help himself, his gaze followed her as she moved back in front of the coffeemaker, dipping to take in the way her jeans hugged her round ass and molded to the curve of her thighs. He gulped and stopped wondering about the Hulk-like sturdiness of his mug and started praying his zipper had been made with the same strength.

"So you put this here, pop in the coffee pod, hit the cup button, and…" The machine, obviously having fallen under her spell, made a hissing noise, and coffee streamed into her mug as she turned to face him. "Voilà, nectar of the gods."

The brilliance of her smile activated every oh-shit alarm he had. This was not the same woman who'd told him to take a flying leap off the tallest peak last night. He narrowed his eyes, trying to see past the lust and sleep deprivation messing with his vision. "What's with the happy helper attitude all of the sudden?"

A flush surged above the V of her sweater, and she nibbled her juicy bottom lip—the one that tasted better than cherries warmed by the sun—but she didn't look away. "I'm shitty at apologies."

"As royalty, I doubt you've had to offer many," he said, still trying to unravel her change in attitude toward him.

She shrugged and took her now full mug from the evil machine, blowing on it, sending a plume of steam toward him. "I haven't been a princess in a long time, and stylists make them all the time, especially for shoppers who don't do casual."

The reminder of his words to her in the Dylan's showroom had his lips curling upward before he could stop himself.

"Last night was…" She paused, giving him a fragile smile that looked about to tremble. "A shock. Really, the whole day was, and I reacted, and acted, badly. I've made it through the past ten years by keeping secrets. I didn't think about tomorrow, because for too long I've been running from a past I couldn't tell anyone about. Getting close to anyone was the most dangerous thing I could do. Compartmentalizing everything, including sex, helped me do that, and to make that work I had to have rules, like no beds, no overnights, no connections."

Fuck. He'd acted like she was only a means to an end and not a person. He'd kidnapped her—for her own good, of course—and now she was making excuses to him for her behavior after he'd gone all horny caveman on her. An uncomfortable and unfamiliar guilt slithered down his spine. "You don't have to tell me this."

"I do." And this time her full lips did tremble, just enough to make him want to reach out, but she let out a sigh and stilled the quiver. "I was a bitch last night, and I'm sorry."

He stiffened, the formality he'd learned growing up on the farthest edge of the royal circle locking his joints into place. "It's not necessary to apologize for not wanting to have sex with me."

She took a sip of her coffee, watching him from over the rim. "I never said I didn't want you."

Her declaration, more challenge than admission, hung in the coffee-scented air between them as he tested out the angles in his head. Her words had the ring of truth, but there was an underlying…something tensing up his gut. She was stirring up trouble, or she was bat-shit crazy. Either option was as likely as the other right now, and neither was helpful to the cause he'd devoted his life to.

"I'm glad we didn't have sex." There was that delicate shrug of hers again. "It would have made the days ahead awkward, since I need you to teach me everything there is to know about Elskov and the plan to get me back on the throne."

That was not what he'd been expecting. Having to sniff his coffee for poison? Yes. Finding a kitchen knife slid up her sleeve? Absolutely. Her simple agreement less than twelve hours after saying she'd think about it? Nope.

"So you're in, huh?" he asked, watching her face as if he could glean what she was hiding.

She didn't even twitch. "I'm here, aren't I?"

"You're here because I stole you away and the Fjende are hot on your trail."

"Are you saying you don't want me to be queen anymore?" She was all big, innocent eyes and unassuming sweetness as she drank her coffee.

"I don't trust your sudden change of heart." Damn, someone really needed to rename him Captain Obvious after his last two statements.

"Fair enough," she said, her voice steady and neutral.

That was it. No denial. No rambling promises. She played her cards so close he'd need to be inside her head to get a look at them. Too bad for her that wasn't going to be a problem. He'd gotten to where he was in the world because no one dissected a problem—made by man or the divine—like he did. She leaned against the counter, obviously willing to wait him out, and traced her fingertip across the top of her mug, as gently as if she was touching a lover. His cock thickened. No doubt it was exactly the result she'd hoped for.

She might be playing, but he wasn't. It didn't get more real than what was going down in four days. Everything depended on it, and he wasn't about to let his dick fuck it up.

He held out his mug to her. "Make me a cup?"

She took the mug and worked her magic on the coffeemaker again before turning to face him. "I'll do it on three conditions."

Yes. Now this was more like the Elle he'd met yesterday. "And those are?"

All business now, the flirtatious vibe disappeared replaced with a steely attitude that reminded him of her father.

"While we're here, you call me Elle."

"Done." He nodded. "What else?"

"I need to know the plan," she said. "The whole thing, not just the parts that involve me. I need to know about security. I need the whole picture."

Since it went against his training to laugh in the face of royalty, he swallowed his amusement. "It doesn't work like that."

"Then I'm not the princess you're looking for," she said, hinting at an addiction to American movies that was well documented in her file.

"Nice try, Obi-Wan." He smirked. "But that doesn't work with me."

"Your choice. You can't force me to take the throne." Elle was as smug as if she had spent her life sitting on the gold throne and wearing the jewel-encrusted crown.

He snorted; he couldn't help himself. "Really?"

"Let me rephrase. You won't force me."

Her confidence poured metaphorical ice water over his head, because she was right. Forty-eight hours ago he could have done it without even a twinge of conscience, but not now. She'd stopped being a symbol and become a person, one with a smart-ass streak a mile wide and who responded so enthusiastically to his caress that it was like touching someone for the first time.

"Interesting theory," he said, his voice sounding strained to his own ears.

"You know it's more than that." She didn't move from her spot lounging against the counter. She didn't need to—her every word was a direct challenge that had him hotter than lava. "I spent the night awake thinking about you, about what you wanted from me, and why. You're not power hungry. You're not maniacal. You're doing the right thing for the right reason, and like a good Elskovian you'll do whatever it takes to win. Pissing off your future queen only hurts your ultimate goal."

She was quick, he'd give her that. While he'd stop short of forcing her sweet ass onto the throne, that left room for a lot of other ways to persuade her to his way of thinking. "I like that you were thinking about me."

Heat flared in her gaze. "The third condition is I want to know what happens to you if this whole thing works out."

Taking a step closer, he left enough space between them that they weren't touching, even though he could feel every delectable inch of her. "When, not if, Princess."

The vein in her throat beat faster as her tongue sneaked out and wet her lips. "All right, what happens to you *when* this is over?"

He reached out, he couldn't help it, and toyed with the cashmere belt that kept her sweater tied shut. "I go back to London knowing the Fjende have been defeated and you're back safe where you belong."

The uptick in her breath. The way her nipples pebbled under the pink sweater. The need coming off her in waves so strong he knew that if he slipped a hand down her jeans he'd find her soaked and ready for him. All of it combined to almost make him forget why they were here in this mountain compound—which was exactly why, instead of pulling the belt so her sweater fell open, he let it slip through his fingers.

"Why would you do so much for a country you never planned to return to?" she asked in a husky, unsure voice.

The caveman part of him, the part that wanted to strip her naked and spread her legs wide so he could taste her again, yowled at the reminder of the real reason they were both here: the plan, the one that couldn't fail. The one he wouldn't let fail. His parents' memory demanded it.

"I can't. I'm a son of Elskov, but not a citizen," he said. "Rich royalist supporters as they were, my parents weren't citizens. That's what would have made them the perfect cover and caretakers for you after the coup."

She picked her mug up from the counter and took a long sip, as if processing his announcement. "After the Kronig, I'll never see you again?"

"Royalty runs in different circles than I do." To put it mildly. He'd worked hard to create the perfect cover, that of the rich, entitled, obnoxiously new-monied Dom Rasmussen, who was always surrounded by starlets, social climbers, and people of dubious morals. His misdeeds and excesses were all lovingly Instagrammed and documented on fans' Tumblrs. He was a social media–savvy Gatsby for the twenty-first century. "If you've read any of the gossip sites, you know I'm beyond socially unacceptable."

"Will the world ever know your part in this?"

"Not if we do this right." And he prayed like hell that's exactly how everything would go down.

She removed his mug from the coffeemaker and held it out to him. "You really are Bruce Wayne."

"You watch too many Hollywood movies." He took his mug, his fingers brushing hers for a brief moment that seared his skin, and held it up in a toast. "Long live the queen." He tapped her mug. "Now let's get to work."

• • •

With three days to go before the Kronig, Elle found herself

sweaty, panting, and flat on her back underneath Dom. Of course, she was fully dressed and in the compound's gym, which took all the fun out of things—at least the kind of fun she imagined every night when she was alone in that mammoth bed with her fingers between her legs. The man was lethal to her self-control.

"Explain to me again why we're doing this?" she asked between heavy breaths as she remained pinned between the thick workout mat and Dom's hard body.

He stood up, planting his feet on each side of her as he reached down to help her up. "Because I won't always be with you."

"And because of that, I have to go to princess pummeling academy?" She took his hand, the now familiar sizzle of electricity arcing between them and jolting her down to her toes, and he yanked her up into a standing position.

He gave her a crooked grin and winked. "Exactly."

Once again, they faced off, circling each other on the red mat. Muscles she didn't even know she had ached from the daily afternoon workouts, and her brain was so full of the latest political gossip about Elskov's most powerful and influential people that it was about to leak out her ears. And when she wasn't getting beaten up, learning how inadequate the self-defense class she'd taken in Harbor City was, or watching yet another PowerPoint presentation about the realities of ruling a country, she was fantasizing about picking up where they'd left off in the library her first night here. Not that he'd made a move in that direction. Oh, he'd flirted as easily as he breathed, but that was it.

She should be glad.

She wasn't.

"This sucks," she muttered as she landed a solid punch to his rock-hard midsection.

He laughed off her effort. "Not as bad as dying."

True story. Death was not part of her plan to get out of here, ditch the throne, and disappear again before the Fjende had a chance to know she was in the wind. "You're smug when you're right." Another jab that he dodged without flinching.

"I guess that means I'm smug all the time." He rested his hands on his narrow hips, his thumbs even with the V-shaped indents along his hips that made her mouth go dry.

Judging by the way his gaze kept flickering between her eyes and her hands, he expected another punch or jab. Taking advantage of the moment, she kicked out her leg, sweeping his out from underneath him. He landed with a solid thump on his ass.

Triumph soothed her aches. "Not so full of yourself now, are you?"

Too late, she felt his fingers close around her ankle. The ground flip-flopped with the ceiling, and she landed on her back. Before she could force the air back in her lungs, Dom straddled her with his knees on either side of her hips. He clasped her wrists and pushed them above her head, trapping her beneath his perfect body covered only by a loose pair of workout shorts. Sweat glistened on his defined pecs, and his biceps bulged. Above her, his blue eyes darkened as his gaze dipped to her mouth.

The air crackled with possibility and promise. Her nipples strained against the cruel confines of her sports bra, and it took everything she had not to moan out loud and grind her hot center against him. Even if she could wriggle free from him, she didn't want to—a recurring motif over the past few days. The more she moved away, the closer she got to him. Over the past few days, she'd learned the compound's layout, familiarized herself with the security personnel and their procedures, and filched a set of car keys and a thick stack of unmarked bills from the kitchen cookie jar. Yet here she was, hoping like hell that he'd rip her pants off and pound into her until she came all over his hard cock. She wanted it despite knowing she shouldn't—maybe for that exact reason—and even with knowing there were surveillance cameras in the room.

"It seems no matter what you do, you keep ending up on your back beneath me."

With his fingers around her wrists as the epicenter, desire spread out over her skin, making her breasts heavy and her core ache. "I have no idea how that happens."

His jaw hardened, the vein at his temple going into overdrive, and time stopped moving. The rest of the world fell away, and her hips arched upward of their own volition, the need for contact overwhelming her better judgment. He was iron against her slick softness. Dom squeezed his brilliant blue eyes closed, glorious torture etched into every line on his face. Then he sprang up to a standing position, his hands fisted.

"You ready to go again?" He settled his stance and let his arms fall loose at his sides.

Pulse racing through her tingling body like a runaway train propelled by a nitro boost, she fought to regain her composure, like she always seemed to be doing around this man. "You've got to be kidding me."

He laughed but didn't come closer, didn't offer her a hand up as he usually did. Looked like she wasn't the only one affected by their constant proximity. A few days ago her plan had been to use that to her benefit. Now she had everything she needed to escape, but she was still here torturing herself by teasing the Viking warrior who meant to lock her away in a castle. What in the hell was wrong with her?

Dom circled her, stalking her as he prepared another attack. "Did I mention this place has its own movie theater and access to almost every movie on the face of the earth?"

She rolled into a sitting position, sweat dripping down

her neck and exhaustion making her limbs heavy now that he wasn't touching her. "That's not fair."

He'd scored a direct hit to her weakest point without a single swing. No one knew her like the Netflix recommendations algorithm. Movies were her drug of choice, especially the old black-and-white romances. When deciding what color to dye her hair as part of her I'm-not-Princess-Eloise disguise, she'd almost gone with Audrey Hepburn black, but with her pale Nordic skin it would have looked more Morticia Addams than Sabrina, so she'd gone with Nancy Drew strawberry blond instead.

"One last go-around and winner gets to pick the movie," he said and set the timer on his cell phone to four minutes.

She leaped up and eyed him for weaknesses; after all, he had to have at least one. "Your ass is mine, Dom."

"Talk dirty to me all you want, Elle, I'm still going to win." He smirked, the corners of his blue eyes crinkling up at the corners, and hit the start button on the timer. "Just like I always do."

Not this time. "We'll see about that."

She lunged. He bobbed and weaved. And so it began again. A few sweaty minutes later, she was standing above Dom, adrenaline coursing through her veins, with her foot resting gently on his windpipe. "I'm sensing a chick flick in your future."

He rolled, and she tumbled. Her cheek ended up flat against the vinyl mat that smelled of Dom—a trademark-worthy combination of pheromones, musk, and a hint of lumberjack—right as the timer went off. "I know exactly what we'll be watching, and it won't be some crappy movie about bridesmaid dresses or missed trains."

She pushed herself up on her hands and knees, sucking in a deep breath, and glanced at him over her shoulder. "Just two hours of shit blowing up?"

His gaze skimmed across her skin, as devastating as his touch. "You'll have to wait to find out."

Giving in to the urge to play with fire, she stretched into downward dog, staying there a moment before transitioning into a standing position. His body tensed, and he fisted his hands as he stared at her, hunger coming off him in waves that battered her.

Three steps. That's all it would take to be close enough to run a palm across his chest. "I don't like waiting," she said, the words referring to more than her curiosity about what movie he'd pick.

His shoulders tightened, and he took half a step forward before stopping abruptly. The heat left his eyes, and his gaze went away from her and over her left shoulder as a neutral mask replaced the flirty smirk he'd had only a heartbeat before.

"In a few days, when you're queen, you won't have to anymore." He dipped his chin in deference and walked out of the sparring circle.

The cool breeze of dismissal chilled her skin, sank underneath and cooled her to the bone. Queen. That thing she'd never wanted or planned to be. The sooner she could shake off whatever was holding her here, the better. She'd give herself one more night. When Dom walked into the library tomorrow morning, he'd find himself without a sovereign. A one-two punch of guilt left her stomach aching, but she couldn't give in—not to exterminate the ghosts she saw in his eyes when he talked about the coup, not to live up to the standards her father had set, not to protect the Elskovians unknowingly supporting a farce of a government. She didn't owe Dom or Elskov anything. And the more she repeated that to herself, the more likely she was to finally have it sink in and take root. But somehow, no matter how many times she told herself that, she couldn't shake the realization that she was only wasting time lying to herself.

"I'm serious about my movies." She grabbed a hand towel and wiped her face to cover her own confusion and indecision. "This better not suck."

"Don't worry," he said. "I never disappoint."

With any luck, she'd find out the truth of that statement herself.

Chapter Eight

This wasn't a date.

Dom dug through the stack of sweaters he owned but never wore for a minute before he found it. Dark blue, it reminded him of the sweater Elle had offered up for him to try on at Dylan's. He hadn't lied; he didn't do casual. The tags were still on the damn wooly thing, and he'd owned it for at least a year. But he also didn't do movie nights or days on end of only his hand for company instead of a woman. He yanked on the sweater with more force than necessary and looked at the result in the floor-to-ceiling mirror. Jeans. He was in fucking jeans and a sweater. It was like he'd turned into an ad for casual lame suburban dad. The slacks and button-down shirts on the hangers called out to him, but he didn't listen, surrendering to the inevitable. She'd gotten under his skin, and now the man who plotted to take down governments was as nervous about his wardrobe as a teenager before the first day of school.

Fucking ridiculous.

He stormed out of the walk-in closet and through his

wood-paneled room without taking a moment to enjoy the breathtaking mountain view, the huge stone fireplace that dominated the south wall, or the oak bed big enough for five women when there was only one he wanted to see naked and twisted in its steel-gray silk sheets. And she wasn't ever going to be there.

For a man who lived by a very specific set of rules, all built around obtaining his one life goal, Elle was the exception to every one. He should back out of movie night. That was the right move, the one that made sense. The one that kept him focused on the plan. The one he wasn't going to make.

He grabbed his cell and dialed the security room. It barely made it through the first ring. "Sir."

"Status report, Major Bendtsen."

"Everything is quiet here, and our sources in Harbor City report the Fjende contingent remains in the city."

Unease crept up Dom's spine. The Fjende weren't the sit-around types. "Have they connected Princess Eloise to Elle Olsen?"

"Unknown, sir."

He tugged at the crew collar of the sweater as heat blasted up from his toes. "We have moles in their organization. What in the hell are we paying them for?"

"The leadership is keeping a tight lid on this one, sir."

Big fucking whoop-de-do. "I want answers. Now. Tell the moles to do whatever it takes to get them."

"Yes, sir."

He disconnected, pocketing his phone as he strode out of the room. The door clicked behind him, his thoughts centered on unwinding the mystery of exactly what angle the Fjende were working. They hadn't given up on finding Elle, and with forty-eight hours until the Kronig, the clock was ticking down.

"Nice sweater," Elle said. "I knew indigo was your color."

His brain braked to a stop so fast his ears rang with the

squealing of rubber against pavement. She was in black jeans that fit like second skin and a T-shirt of the same color that hung off one bare shoulder. Then the fact that a bra strap wasn't showing registered in his already lust-fogged brain, and the little things like remembering to breathe became a hardship.

Standing outside her door, she took her time looking him up and down, and it took everything he had not to gather her up and carry her back to his oversize bed. By the time her heavy-lidded gaze had made its way back up to his face, his entire body was on fire. The woman was going to kill him.

"So what's the movie?" she asked, her eyes hooded with lust.

"You have to wait and find out." He laid his palm against the small of her back, relishing how she relaxed into his touch.

They walked in silence to the movie room in the basement, every unspoken word a current running between them. A large screen took up almost one entire wall, the Paramount Pictures logo in black and white paused on the screen. Facing it were small leather couches on risers. The staff had put a tub of popcorn as well as an array of candy and sodas on the table next to the center front-row love seat.

"Wow." She let out a low whistle. "This is heaven."

"Glad you approve."

"You have no idea."

They sat in the designated love seat. There was more than enough room for both of them. He grabbed the remote and pushed the green button. The back of the seat tilted, and a footrest rose up from beneath them.

"I might never leave."

"If I'd known a night at the movies was all it took to make you this pliable, I would have brought you here right away."

"You'll have to remember that tidbit for the next princess you kidnap."

He hit the blue button, and the lights dimmed. "I'm hoping you'll be my first and last princess kidnapping."

"Sounds like a plan." She set the popcorn tub between them and grabbed a handful. "Enough stalling—movie time."

He tapped the red button and watched her from the corner of his eye as the credits rolled. The movie he'd picked was a gamble. If she took it the wrong way, he was fucked.

"Dom." She half sighed his name. "*Roman Holiday* is my favorite."

Only then did he relax back into the plush seat. Included in her dossier was an ever-growing spreadsheet of her Netflix movie history. *Roman Holiday* had more entries than any other. Still, he hadn't picked the story of a runaway princess who has to decide between a regular life and her duty to the crown lightly. She still wasn't totally on board with the Resistance's plan. With any luck, Elle would make the same decision as the movie princess.

. . .

Throat burning and her bottom lip quaking, Elle held her breath as she watched the reporter walk alone down the marble hallway, his lonely steps echoing. The princess wasn't going to come back and tell him she loved him, she couldn't. He was a commoner, and she was a princess. She'd made her decision to do her duty and sit on her country's throne. They'd never see each other again. And it was the right choice. She owed it to her country and her people to remain on the throne—like Elle's father had, like she'd always known he would.

Before he'd been killed, she'd begged him to go somewhere safe, but he wouldn't leave his home, his people. "We owe this country everything," he'd said, wiping away her tears. "It is not our right, it is our duty, and it comes before everything, Eloise, everything."

The memory settled in her stomach like a lead weight. Less than twenty-four hours later he'd been dead, but like the princess in the movie, he'd made the right choice to stay. He would have hated himself for the rest of his life if he hadn't. Not just because it was his duty, but because it was the right thing to do. And her father had raised her to always do the right thing.

Inhaling a shaky breath, she filled her lungs until the stolen car key tucked into her bra poked hard into her breast. Two days ago, she'd sneaked the pilfered money and a change of clothes down to the garage, but had kept the Mercedes key fob on her at all times in case the opportunity arose to make a quick escape. In reality, that moment had come and gone several times since then. She'd never taken it…her breath whooshed out of her…and she never would. Running away from her duty wasn't the right choice. Like father, like daughter, like movie princess who chose duty over freedom.

Elle couldn't deny her country when it needed her. She'd never be able to honor her father's memory if she did. The screen went black, and the lights came up.

"That was emotional blackmail." She sniffled and swiped the back of her hand across her damp cheeks.

Dom didn't even bother to look innocent. "What do you mean?"

"Like you just happened to pick *that* movie out of the eleventy billion movies out there?" She snagged the tub of popcorn and grabbed the last bits of salty, buttery goodness. There was no eating like emotional eating. If she had some Mike and Ikes she could really get the party started. "You're about as subtle as a slobbering Labrador with a tennis ball."

"Subtlety wouldn't get my message through." He curled his fingers around her chin and tugged so she faced him, a frisson of attraction dancing across her skin at his touch.

"So are you going to return the keys to the Mercedes and the kitchen's rainy-day money and follow through with your promise?"

Her stomach slid out her toes. "You knew."

"Of course." He dragged his thumb across her bottom lip with a roughness that added just enough friction to make her catch her breath.

"Were you going to try to stop me?" she asked as she twisted in the seat, brushing her knee across his as she turned to face him completely and opened her mouth so she could graze her teeth across the rough pad of his thumb still pressed to her lip.

The vein in his temple throbbed, and his jaw tightened. "I've already told you, trying isn't an option."

He dwarfed her—his warm hand so large against her jaw and his broad shoulders blocking out the rest of the room. She kissed the spot on his thumb where her teeth had been. Hard and soft. Bite and caress. Need and denial. That was them in a nutshell. And this push and pull between them that had nearly knocked her to her knees the first time she saw him? It scared her almost as much as the realization that she'd be taking back her crown.

"Is there anything that matters more to you than getting me on the throne?"

He dropped his hand, her question seemingly the reminder he needed that he shouldn't be touching his queen. Still, he didn't move back, didn't inch his knee away from hers.

"No." There wasn't a trace of doubt or hesitation in his answer. It was like she'd asked if the sky was neon pink.

She slid her hand inside her loose T-shirt and plucked the key fob out of her strapless bra. "Give me your hand." He held out his hand, palm up, and she pressed the key into its center, closing his strong fingers around it. "You've got your queen."

The nausea she expected never rose in her throat. Her palms didn't become clammy. And for the first time since the coup, she knew what was coming next and the part she'd play. Finally, her destiny was her own.

Dom stood up, and she had to crane her neck to take all of him in from her sitting position. The man knew how to fill out a pair of jeans and a fisherman's sweater. Thick thighs. High, round ass, broad chest, and thick, corded forearms visible where he'd pushed the sleeves up. It wasn't just his muscular build, though; it was the stubborn tilt to his chin, the confidence shining in his blue eyes, and the aura of power that emanated from him every time he so much as breathed.

Plain and simple, she wanted him, and this would be the last few days of her life when she could have what she wanted without worrying about how it fit into her life as queen. For the next two days, they weren't the billionaire commoner and the future queen with the same likelihood of being together as the princess and the reporter in *Roman Holiday*. For a little bit longer, she could be just a woman and he could be the man who rocked her world.

"You're staring," he said, his tone gruff with want, pulling her attention to his handsome face.

"I know." Liquid heat flowed through her, and she let her gaze skim across his body, her mouth watering with want of him. "We have less than forty-eight hours. I suggest we take advantage of it."

There went that vein at his temple again. "What's your proposal?"

She slipped her hand under her shirt, reaching around behind for the hooks holding her strapless bra closed, loving the soft growl of a groan he made as he watched. "Our own Roman holiday, but with more naked and fewer tourist attractions."

"After that you go back to your royal duties." He stepped

closer, putting her practically within licking distance of his hard cock fighting against the confines of his jeans.

"Exactly." More words weren't possible right now. She was surprised she got a three-syllable word out, considering the trouble she was having unhooking her bra, an action she'd done a million times before.

Finally, it gave, and her boobs swung free, her stiff nipples pushing against the soft cotton of her T-shirt. She slid the bra out from underneath her shirt, dropping the black lace lingerie where Dom had sat only minutes before. Then she looked up at him through the fringe of her lashes and teased her full bottom lip with the edge of her teeth.

His jaw tightened even as his cock twitched under the thick denim. "I'm not an easy man, not even for forty-eight hours."

Keeping her gaze locked on his face, she stroked the hard outline of his dick with the tip of her fingernail. "Good thing I like things hard."

He grabbed her wrists and pulled her toward him, his face an icy mask of control when she knew how hot he burned for her. The intensity of it should have frightened her. Instead, it left her panting for more as her body ached for his touch.

"There won't be a repeat of what happened in the library," he said in a low tone as he held her arms aloft, his grip tight but not cruel. "When it's the two of us and that pussy of yours is soft, swollen, and wet, I'll be the one in control. I'll have you wherever and whenever I want—in my bed, on my desk, on the floor right now if I want to. I'm going to own that sexy body of yours so thoroughly that you're going to beg for my cock, because it's going to be the only thing in the world that you want. And once I'm buried balls deep in you and you are filled with me, I'm going to make you come apart in the best way possible. Do you understand?"

"Yes." The single word came out half promise, half plea

as she clenched her thighs tight, almost convinced she could come just from the mix of pressure and his words.

"Say it." He jerked her arms high and back, forcing her to arch her spine so her breasts jutted out.

Thrill shivered up her body. "I understand."

"What do you understand?" He lowered one hand and drew lazy circles around her still covered nipples, too soft to be what she needed and too hard to be ignored.

Her pussy quivered as she watched his long finger trace a figure eight as it traveled from one nipple to the other. He loomed over her, bold, fierce, and commanding, with only one thing on his mind—her. It was almost enough to make her orgasm on the spot. Almost. But first she had to make sure he understood her ground rules.

"I understand that for the next forty-eight hours this pussy is yours to play with, this body is yours to touch, and this mouth is yours to plunder." Pushing against his hold, she leaned forward enough to glide her lips over his denim-covered cock as he moaned his appreciation. "Just remember your dick is mine to ride, your body is mine to taste, and your mouth is mine to tease, tempt, and enjoy. I'm not easy, either."

"No queen should be." He pulled her up, sliding her body against his as she rose. "But you're not queen yet."

His mouth crashed down on hers. Calling it a kiss would be a misnomer. A claiming. A guarantee. A threat. Fuck, it was heaven and hell mixed together with enough sensual promise to make it so Elle didn't care where she ended up, as long as she was with Dom.

Chapter Nine

This was a mistake, and Dom didn't give a shit. Elle had gotten to him with the boldness inherent in her every move and the sway of her sweet ass in those jeans. She'd be an untouchable queen in a few days, but for the next forty-eight hours she was his—all of her, from her silky reddish-blond hair to her bee-stung lips to her dick-hardening curves and the extra little I-dare-you jauntiness in her hip-swaying walk.

He threaded his hands through her thick hair, cupping the back of her head, and deepened the kiss. God, she tasted of buttery popcorn, sour apples, and perfection. Oh, Elle wasn't perfect, future queen or not, but right now, at this moment, the two of them were as close to it as they'd ever get. He wasn't about to waste a minute of the next two days.

Desperate to devour more of her, he tore his mouth away, missing the divine torment of her lips the millisecond he broke contact. "Fuck me," he groaned against the delicate curve of her jaw.

Her throaty chuckle vibrated against his tongue as he licked and kissed his way down her neck. "I was hoping you'd let me do that."

A soft nip of her tender flesh turned her teasing words into a sultry moan. "Begging already, Elle?"

"You wish," she said, her voice breathy, but with the underlying provocation he'd come to expect from her.

He tightened his grip on her hair, pulling the strawberry silk strands, forcing her face upward, and giving himself better access to the long column of her throat. "Always a challenge with you."

"I know you can't resist."

"You're right." He trailed his lips across her shoulder, left bare by the wide neck of her T-shirt. "I can't resist you."

Her hands weren't idle. She sneaked underneath his sweater, her fingers tormenting his chest with a light touch that had him craving more. He wanted, needed, all of her. Now. There wasn't time to waste. She didn't have to worry about breaking her no-beds rule, at least not yet, because they weren't going to make it out of the home theater.

Cupping her ass, he lifted her so she fit snug against him, so soft where he was so damn hard, and strode across the room to the intercom. He pressed Elle against the wall and jabbed the talk button.

"Yes, sir," Major Bendtsen said.

"Turn off the video feed."

He didn't wait for an answer. He didn't need to. His orders weren't ever ignored.

"That was subtle." She wrapped her long legs around his waist as her hands continued to explore him underneath his sweater. "Would you like to send out a Resistance-wide memo letting everyone know you're about to bang me?"

Mouthy. He liked that. He liked her, the way she didn't back down and always found a way to keep fighting. "Is that what I'm going to do?"

"Sure feels like it." She undulated, her slick warmth

seeping through her pants as she ground against him.

Pleasure spiraled outward from his dick until his whole body vibrated with white-hot need. That's it. She was going to kill him, and he was going to die a happy man. "How fast can you get naked?"

Adding the right amount of pressure to her touch to make his cock twitch, she grazed her fingernails down his chest. "Put me down and find out."

She didn't have to say it twice.

• • •

Her feet were on the ground before she could take another breath.

"Strip." His demand was as hard as he was.

"Haven't you already seen that show?" she teased, loving how it made that vein in his temple pulse.

He lifted an eyebrow. The sexy bastard knew full well she was provoking him. "Some things are worth seeing again."

Exhilaration swept through her like wildfire, melting away every part of her she'd kept frozen and in check. He did this to her when no one else ever had. She stuck her thumbs into the waistband of her pants and shimmied them down her hips, just enough that he could see she was totally bare underneath. "Why don't you take a seat and we can do this right this time?"

Dom stalked over to the leather love seat, removed the empty tub of popcorn, and sat down. His hand fell over the bulge in his jeans, and he gave it a few lazy strokes. "That's your one."

"My one?"

A dangerous glint came into those arctic-blue eyes of his. "The one time you get to call the shots."

"So if I tell you to lick here." She pushed her leggings

down lower, exposing herself and basking in the lavalike heat of his gaze. "You wouldn't?"

"No." So firm, so confident.

Oh, they'd see about that. She turned, presenting him with her bare ass as she bent over with her legs straight and slid the material down to her ankles. Widening her stance a bit, she looked over her shoulder at him. An amused smile curled his sinfully full lips, but that wasn't what made her heart double-time. It was the way he held himself absolutely still, his focus locked on her, as if it was taking everything he had not to bound off the love seat and fuck her right there on the floor while she was half naked and trembling with want. She almost moaned out loud at the sight before remembering that, like always, she needed to keep a mental distance. Sex was sex. With Dom it would be dirtier, hotter, and better than most, but she couldn't get lost in him, couldn't feel safe. He wasn't her forever—he was her *Roman Holiday*.

Free of her pants, she turned back to face him, pulling her thin T-shirt down in the middle to stop him from getting a good look at exactly what he wanted to see. The move made the material slide farther off her shoulder, exposing her breast right down to the top curve of her light pink areola. His jaw went hard. She got even wetter but didn't speed up this striptease. She couldn't help herself—she wanted to know how far she could push him before he lost his iron grip on control.

She wet her lips, a quick flick of her tongue that left her mouth glistening. A little nonverbal suggestion never hurt anyone. "So how do I get you to lick me?"

"All you have to do is ask," he said, his voice low and full of decadent promise, his wicked words fire on her already sensitive skin.

"And you'll say yes?" Her core clenched at the possibility.

A predatory grin curled the corners of his delicious

mouth. "Depends on how pretty you put it."

Trouble, thy name is Dom. And it was just the kind of trouble she liked, what had pulled her to him the moment he'd stepped off the elevator onto the Dylan's showroom floor. Big risk, big reward. Her gaze dipped down to the outline of his hard cock against his jeans. Her mouth went dry, and her nipples stiffened to almost painful peaks.

"You want me to beg." Damn, how had her voice gotten that breathy and needy?

"I want to make you so hot you won't be able to make a coherent sound at all." He reached behind his head and pulled off the sweater, revealing a wide plane of muscle dusted with light blond hair that became several shades darker as it formed a line that disappeared behind his waistband. "Now take off the shirt."

It was there in his tone, that loose string that if she pulled it he'd come undone. Anticipation thrummed through her body and soul. She tugged the shirt farther down, and one stiff nipple popped out of the top. "This shirt?"

He leaned forward, letting his forearms rest on his muscular thighs, his hands hanging loose as if the tension between them wasn't gripping both of them tight. "Last warning, Elle."

"Or what?" She batted her eyelashes at him, coy as could be. "You'll spank me?"

"No." A flash of something hard, determined, and so hungry for her it defied description crossed his face. "That shirt will come off anyway, and then I'll take you right to the edge of coming and stop. Then I'll do that again and again and again until you're so slippery with want that you really will beg me to give you what you need."

How she kept her legs from collapsing, she wasn't sure. "And will you?"

"Eventually." He relaxed back into the love seat, like a

panther toying with its prey. "*If* you're a good girl." He paused, his gaze devouring her. "Take it off. Now."

Too turned on to delay any longer, she whipped her shirt off and stood naked before him. "Happy now?"

"Getting there." He squeezed his cock through his jeans. "Come over here."

On wobbly legs, she did. He stretched his arms across the back of the love seat, giving her a prime view of his magnificent bare chest. "Take off my jeans."

Unable to deny him—or herself—any longer, she practically leaped at the chance. Her hands trembled as she snapped open the button and lowered his zipper. He lifted his hips, and she tugged the jeans off. She almost came on the spot. He was commando.

"Since you're so interested in licking, Elle, why don't you start?"

It wasn't a command. It wasn't a request. It was a challenge. He wanted to play…and so did she.

Settling down on her knees, she wrapped her fingers around the base of his cock. It was hot silk wrapped around iron. Bringing it up to her mouth, she looked up to see him watching her. Good. She was going to put on a show. Time to make Mr. Control Freak let go. She started soft. Just the tip of her tongue against his head, little lapping tastes at the precome that had him closing his eyes in ecstasy. It was meant to make him crazy, but it had the same effect on her. She couldn't get enough. The head, the base, the shaft, she licked it all before taking him deep into her mouth and then releasing him and starting all over again with teasing licks around the head.

"Elle," he groaned.

Pulling back, she grinned and sat on her heels. "Are you begging, Dom?"

Something dangerous sparked in his eyes, and he lifted

her from the floor and slid her up the hard planes of his body until her breasts were at mouth level. "I never beg."

"We'll see about—" The rest died on her lips the moment he took her nipple into his mouth.

Grazing his teeth across the sensitive bud, he teased and tormented her with the same lazy, determined ease that she had used on him until she was ready to agree to anything if he promised to never stop. But he did.

He twisted so her back was flat against the leather still warm from him. "Lie back and let's see what sounds that smart mouth of yours makes when you come all over my tongue."

Elle did and held her breath in anticipation, but instead of diving in, Dom stood up and went to the end of the love seat. He grabbed her ankles and yanked her down so her ass was lifted up on to love seat's arm, then knelt between her splayed legs.

"I've been dreaming about tasting you again." He dragged the rough pad of his thumb across her center.

"What, no foreplay?" She meant it to be casual; it came out desperate for release.

He laughed, his warm breath breezing across her slick folds. "You want me to ignore this beautiful pussy right now?"

"God, no," she groaned.

"Then let's get to the sweet stuff."

He did. His tongue—his magic fucking tongue—claimed her as he licked and sucked and teased her slick folds. Each twist of his pointed tongue around her clit made her thighs vibrate. Every flat-tongued lap across her entrance had her whole body tightening in anticipation. Then he slid his hands from the inside of her thighs to her ass and lifted her lower half up in the air. The new angle partnered with the increased intensity of his tongue sent her over the edge into a free fall of pleasure that left her gasping for breath.

• • •

Watching Elle come down from orgasm was almost as good as watching her get there. The extra pink in her cheeks, the way her tits heaved as she caught her breath, and the slow, satisfied curl of her luscious lips had him hard enough to pound nails into concrete. Fuck, he couldn't wait any longer to get inside her. He gathered her orgasm-limp body up and draped her over the back of the love seat so her butt was high in the air and her pussy was at the perfect height for him to slide home. Circling his cock with one hand, he gave it two slow strokes as he admired the smooth lines of her back and how her waist dipped in before flaring out into rounded hips.

Flipping her hair over one shoulder, she turned her head and looked back at him. "Tell me you're not going to just stare at me."

"Such a smart mouth." He spread her legs wide and then the creamy globes of her ass, separating them so he could see how slick she was for him.

"You didn't object to it earli—"

He slid the head of his cock across her plump folds, testing his own control as he teased her, and she let out a sweet moan. He loved those little noises she made when he touched her, the sighs, the cries, the pleas for more.

"Dom." She moved against him as if trying to impale herself on him. "Please."

The urge to drive forward and sink himself in so deep his balls bounced against her clit was like a booming alarm blaring through his body loud enough to make him shake. He didn't have much time before he lost the fight. "Say it," he managed to get out between clenched teeth as he grabbed a condom from the pocket of his jeans lying on the love seat and tore it open.

"Give me your cock," she said. "I need to feel you inside

me."

Fuck. He wasn't sure whether to beat his chest in triumph or fall to his knees and worship her, because Dom had never wanted any woman as much as he wanted Elle. The woman didn't just undo him—she put him back together again.

Holding his breath, he unrolled the condom onto his rock-hard cock and inched into her tightness. He wanted to take his time, remember everything about this moment, about her, but as soon as she gripped him with her warm wetness, he knew it wasn't in the cards. It was too good, too right, too… everything, and he gave in to the chaos she inspired inside him.

"Elle, I can't," he groaned out his weakness.

"Then don't." She pushed back against him, engulfing him inside her and making the rest of the world disappear in one fluid undulation. "Just fuck me, Dom."

Her words broke something inside him, and he pounded into her. Control became a hazy memory as he let go and fucked her like he'd wanted to do from the first moment he'd seen her at Dylan's—hard, fast, thorough, and with the determined desperation of a man who'd been given a limited-time pass to heaven. In and out, he plunged into her, his hands gripping the forgiving flesh of her hips as she milked his dick with her slick walls, giving as good as she got and answering every retreat of his body with an attack of her own. He wasn't the only one lost to the mind-obliterating desire.

Leaning forward so his body partially covered hers, the new angle let him go deep, giving her every inch of him as he slid his arm around her waist and pulled her hard back to him. She cried out her pleasure, calling out his name, and she clenched his cock as her orgasm ripped through her.

It was more than he could take. One, two, three more strokes, and his balls pulled up tight to his body as his own climax roared to the forefront, making him blind to everything but the exquisite release of coming inside Elle. His entire body shaking, he laid his forehead on the damp expanse of her back. She smelled of sweat, sex, and all the unobtainable things in the world that he'd never wanted until now. Women. Wealth. Success. Everything but Elle. It had all come easily to him, and he'd been satisfied, letting his quest for restoring the monarchy to Elskov feed his unending hunger for challenge. But this woman? He inhaled her unique scent. She had him thinking that he could use more challenge in his life. Dangerous thoughts, indeed.

"Unless your goal is to smush me into this love seat, you'd better let me up." She giggled.

He snapped back into a standing position and helped her up. "Sorry about that."

She grabbed her T-shirt and slipped it over her head, leaving her gorgeous tits swinging free underneath, and grinned at him. "You're a dangerous man."

"What makes you say that?" He snagged his jeans and pulled them up, hating the thick denim material that would separate him from her smooth skin.

She tugged on her pants, letting out a hard breath that sent the reddish hair that had flopped in front of her eyes back into place. "Because I just came so hard that I'd agree to eat peanut butter and jelly for a week, and I hate peanut butter."

"What kind of person hates peanut butter?" In the process of pulling on his sweater, his words came out muffled.

She giggled again, and her eyelids drooped lower, a satisfied smile curling her full lips. "The totally-jellified-right-now kind."

He scooped her up, her body light in his arms. "Come on, let's go upstairs and I'll explain the delicacy that is peanut butter."

"I can walk, you know," she said as she snuggled against

him, her palm covering his still fast-beating heart.

"But this way I can guarantee you end up exactly where I want."

"And where's that?" she asked, her eyes fluttering shut.

"My bed." At least for the next forty-eight hours. After that he'd walk away like the reporter in *Roman Holiday*. The thought was a hard kick to his kidneys.

Her body tensed, and he waited for her objection, but none came. Instead, she relaxed by degrees against him as he walked out of the movie room and up the stairs to his room. By the time they'd reached his door, her eyes had fluttered shut, her soft, sleepy breaths tickled his neck, and she felt so right in his arms he wasn't sure he'd ever be able to let go.

Chapter Ten

Elle stretched out on the bed and rolled to her side, snuggling up with Dom's pillow. He'd gotten up half an hour ago when the sun was low in the east and she could barely open her eyes, but she could still smell him on the pillowcase—warm and tempting and better than she'd imagined he'd be. And she had a damn good imagination.

The smell and her memories weren't as good as the real thing. She cracked her eyelids. Rumpled sheets? Check. Super-manly room in dark colors and zero throw pillows? Check. Dom? No check. She sat up and pushed the rat's nest off her face, amazed at how a night of great sex could do serious damage to her hair. Where was he? That's when she saw the note propped up on the bedside table.

> *I'LL BE RIGHT BACK. IN THE KITCHEN, MAKING BREAKFAST. WANT TO MAKE SURE YOU HAVE PLENTY OF ENERGY FOR THE DAY. DON'T MOVE. —D*

Yeah, that was totally going to happen. She grabbed one

of Dom's white button-up shirts off the end of the bed and pulled it on. It came down to midthigh and smelled like him. She then hustled out of the bedroom, dying to know what Dom in the kitchen looked like. It was so unexpected for a billionaire who'd grown up wealthy and never had to make his own breakfast in his life. Was he a secret gourmand? A total newb? Did he make scrambled eggs or quiche? Dry cereal or pancakes? Was it—

She skidded to a stop outside the door to the huge gourmet kitchen. Her tongue turned to sawdust. Even wearing just his crisp dress shirt she was overdressed. He was in boxer briefs—and only boxer briefs—that left absolutely nothing to the imagination. If she'd been wearing panties they would have been toast.

"You going to stand there and ogle my ass, or are you going to help me figure out how in the hell this thing works?" He pointed at the toaster oven.

It took her a second, but she remembered how to breathe and move again. She walked into the kitchen and snuggled up behind him, wrapping her arms around his lean waist and letting her fingertips slip underneath the waistband of his blue boxer briefs. God, he smelled good first thing in the morning. A girl could get used to this—*she* could get used to him, and she couldn't let herself do that. She only had him until the plane left for Elskov, and if that thought wasn't enough to snap her back to reality and step away from Dom before she fell too deep, nothing was.

Heart pounding against her ribs in pre–anxiety attack mode, she took a calming breath and came around to his side. The only thing in front of the toast was a half-empty carton of eggs. No bread. No bagels. No breakfast pizza boxes.

"What are you making?" she asked.

He punched a few buttons on the toaster oven, his nose scrunched up in frustration. Nothing happened. "Scrambled eggs."

As soon as his words penetrated the lust-induced fog that seemed to surround her whenever she was near him, she jumped between Dom and the toaster oven, her finger pressing against one well-developed pec. "Step away from the appliances or you'll kill us all."

"What?" One blond eyebrow went up as he stepped forward, backing her up until her ass was against the counter and his hard body was pressing against her from the front. "I used to make them like this all the time at university."

Desire careened through her. It was wild, breathtaking, and totally out of control. Unable to stop herself from touching him, she circled his flat nipple before leaning in and lapping at the now hard nub with her tongue then sneaking under his impressive biceps. He pivoted, resting his hip against the counter, but didn't chase. He didn't need to. He caressed her just by looking in her direction.

It shouldn't be like this, not with him. He was too dangerous. Too controlled. Too much. But if not Dom, then who could it be like this with? She was going to be queen. In a few years, if the Fjende didn't kill her first, she'd marry an appropriate aristocrat, not a panty-drenching billionaire who wasn't even Elskovian, let alone of the right class. After that, she'd produce an heir who'd follow in her footsteps right onto the throne. There wasn't a space on her royal calendar for Dom. But she wasn't queen yet.

She glanced at the clock and did the math in her head. Thirty-five hours until their private jet took off for Elskov and the rest of her life, if the men who killed her father didn't get to her first. Barbwire knots formed in her stomach. God, what she wouldn't give for her father to be there now. Not so she wouldn't have to be queen, but because he'd know what to do next. He always had. She rubbed her palm on her stomach and pretended the ache was hunger pains.

Dom cocked his head to one side and gave her a considering look. "Hey, you okay?"

"You make eggs in a toaster oven?" she asked, trying to get her brain to focus on breakfast instead of the uncertainty awaiting her in Elskov.

He opened his mouth as if he was going to ask again, closed it, and then shook his head before pointing to the toaster oven. "If I could figure out how to power this thing up, you'll see."

Giving the toaster oven a good look, she spied the problem. "Think this would help?" She held up the unplugged cord.

"We're saved," he sang out in a deep bass, kissed her on the tip of her nose, and plugged in the toaster oven.

It buzzed to life, and a deep orange glow traveled along the coils holding up the ramekins full of eggs. She did a hip-shimmy happy dance. Celebrating successes, even the small ones, was an important way she'd kept her sanity when she'd built her secret identity.

"So what other secret cooking talents do you have?" she asked.

"I'm fucking fantastic at peanut butter and jelly." He narrowed his eyes at her, folding his arms across his chest and making his biceps bulge. "Anyway, you're supposed to be in bed."

"I'm sure both of us are about to be glad I'm not." She wandered over to the pantry and opened it up. "Where is the staff?"

The security staff and handful of others were usually there, even if she only rarely spotted them. She wasn't sure if it was Dom's orders or just the trappings of royalty that she'd have to get used to, knowing she was being watched even in a room by herself.

"Kitchen staff has the morning off."

She grabbed a canister of flour and looked through the rest of the staples for what she needed. "And security?"

"They're about." He shrugged, seemingly satisfied to watch her as she dug through the pantry.

"And that's all you have to say about that." Had she expected more detail because they'd slept together? A small part of her had. Time to squash that expectation, and all expectations about Dom. "You know, all of this controlling-the-information flow is going to get your ass in hot water one of these days."

There was that grin, the one that made her stomach fall to her knees. "Are you going to lecture me or help us make something to go with my fantastic scrambled eggs?"

"Oh, forgive me, Chef Dom." She set the flour, salt, and a few other staples on the island. "Pancakes or waffles?"

He crossed to the island and looked through her gathered ingredients. "Are there chocolate chips?"

"Really?" She raised herself up onto her tiptoes and kissed him. It was supposed to be a brief, silly, you-make-me-laugh kind of kiss, but by the time he broke it off and stepped back, she'd forgotten all of that and maybe her name and age, too. "Are there cameras in here?"

He nodded, his gaze locked on her kiss-swollen lips as his palms glided from her waist to the curve of her hips. God, this man had her thinking about saying *fuck it* and seeing if they could fit in the narrow pantry. A quick glance confirmed that wasn't going to happen.

"I fucking hate your commitment to security." She sighed.

"I'm beginning to agree." He kissed his way down her throat, stopping at that sensitive spot where her neck met her shoulder that turned off her brain with the efficiency of flicking a switch. A light nip, and he backed away. "Okay, pancakes first, then back up to my room, where cameras are banned, and then I will deliver on the promise I made."

"Oh, yeah, which one was that?"

He swept her hair back, exposing her ear, and leaned in close. "To make you scream my name while your toes curl."

A shiver worked its way from her earlobe to deep in her core, and she clenched her thighs together. "We better cook fast."

The corner diner near Dylan's in Harbor City that put fresh pancakes on the table in less than five minutes wasn't going to have a thing on her. She glanced at the clock as the minute hand ticked forward.

• • •

Dom demolished most of the eggs and the stack of pancakes with their buttery-crispy edges without tasting a single one. It was hard to when he'd spent the past hour in the same room as Elle, who was dressed in one of his shirts and nothing else. He'd discovered that tidbit when she'd bent over to get the skillet for the pancakes and the shirt had risen high enough to show the bottom curve of her bare ass. It seemed sporting a boner for this long killed his sense of taste.

He couldn't remember the last time he'd had breakfast with someone he'd slept with. Shit, he couldn't remember the last time he'd *wanted* to have breakfast with someone after a night spent twisting the sheets.

She stabbed a piece of pancake and used it to sop up the last of the swirl of maple syrup on her plate. She pointed the fork at him, syrup dripping from the pancake square impaled on its tines. "I've never seen someone eat pancakes that fast."

"You make pancakes for a lot of people?" he asked, only the fact that he already knew the answer keeping him from bending his fork in half in insane and misplaced jealousy at the possibility.

"No." The light in her big, brown eyes dimmed. "You're

the first."

Her obvious sadness was a punch in the gut. She'd been abandoned, that's what she'd said over and over since they'd gotten to the chalet. He knew her file better than his company's balance sheet—and he could recite that from memory. She'd made the best of a shitty situation, but she'd isolated herself. Ten years of lies, of always looking over her shoulder... It had to have marked her even if she hadn't really been alone, not one single moment.

Guilt morphed the pancakes in his stomach, turning them from fluffy lightness into cement bricks. Clever, determined, snarky, and sexy as hell, she was going to make one hell of a queen, he had to admit, even if she was the woman who made him wish the monarchy didn't exist. For almost ten years, he'd been her invisible shadow, celebrating her successes and mourning her losses from the sidelines as he'd watched in awe while she made a place for herself in a strange new world.

In a parallel world where the coup had never happened and his being a commoner didn't matter, things might have turned out differently. Falling in love with her wasn't a possibility, but Dom wasn't sure he had the choice. What he did have a choice about was telling her the truth—or at least as much of it as he could.

"Elle, I need to tell you something."

She flashed a sassy grin, put her fork on her now-empty plate, and leaned forward, giving him enough of a view of her perfect tits to make his brain short-circuit. "Is it that you're madly in love with me and you want to run away to a private island where we'll live out our days naked and happy?"

"I like the sound of that." In fact, he already had the island.

"Don't even joke." She stuck out her tongue and giggled, but the smile in her voice didn't reach her eyes. "You're the Gregory Peck reporter character in this situation. You have to walk away alone at the end, and I have to do my duty."

That hurt more than it should. "No island?"

"Nope, we're each on our own. Lucky for me I've got a decade's worth of experience on that front." She casually sipped her coffee, but there was no missing the slight shake to the mug in her hands. "So, what did you really need to say?"

"You weren't alone." Shit. He hadn't meant to blurt it out like that.

She set her mug down with a *clank*, and her eyes narrowed. "The guys I went home with. You knew about them. You said you were at the bar."

Fuck. So much for being Mr. Smooth. "Yes."

She went still and stared at him. He gulped and shifted on the tall bar stool. Here he was, a billionaire poised to overthrow a government, and she had him squirming in his seat.

"What else?"

Feeling the sharp corner of each guilt-formed concrete brick jabbing against his stomach lining, he sighed and straightened his shoulders. He'd opened the door, now it was time to walk through it. "It took us almost a year to track you down after you'd gotten to America. Lucky for us we knew you were landing in Harbor City, so we had a starting point."

"Nine years?" she asked, her voice sharp enough to be considered a weapon. "You, the Resistance, have known where I was for nine years?" She smacked her hand against the granite island, her eyes damp and her lip trembling. "All that time I thought I was alone and you knew where I was and never came forward?"

Yep, his stomach was shredded. He could take tears. He couldn't take hers, not after he'd seen for himself how much spirit she had. Taking a shot at him. Fighting with all she had in the workout room. The stubborn determination not to be pushed into a decision but to choose her destiny herself, for her own reasons. That Elle wouldn't be broken; he'd kill the person who tried. But when it came to everything that had happened before he walked out of the elevator and onto the showroom floor at Dylan's, he hadn't had a choice.

"The Fjende knew about us and were looking for you. If we had made overt contact, they would have found you. We were there as much as we could be."

"What do you mean?"

Okay, fuck this. For each degree she cooled, he only heated up. Maybe it was the guilt. Maybe it was because he had done everything he could. Probably it was both.

"Your apartment? I own it. That's why the rent hasn't gone up in eight years." His frustration at himself leaked into his voice, turning it hard and heated. "Your full-ride scholarship to the Fashion Institute of Harbor City? My company sponsored it." He needed to reel the emotion back in, but he couldn't when it came to her. He never could. So he plowed forward, his voice getting louder with each word. "Mrs. Beeman who lives in the apartment below yours and always brings you soup in the winter and asks you to watch her Pomeranian? She's one of ours. We've always been there."

He had done his best. Facing her as she blinked those big, brown eyes fast and furious to stop the tears from flowing, it felt like it hadn't been enough.

Looking anywhere but at him, she toyed with her coffee mug, spinning it around and around with shaking fingers. The hollow sound of ceramic turning on granite echoed in the suddenly quiet kitchen. The urge to keep talking, to keep proving himself, burned him up, but giving in wasn't an option. Pushing her never gained the results he wanted—he'd learned that the hard way the day they'd arrived at the chalet and she'd tried to blow his head off.

Finally, she righted the mug and folded her hands into her lap before looking him straight in the eyes. "Is there anything else?"

His gut churned. More? Oh, fuck, yes, there was. "What do you mean?"

"If you've been keeping other secrets, now's the time to share."

Just little things, like the fact that her father was alive and the Resistance's leader. He could tell her. Shit, he *wanted* to tell her, but he couldn't break his vow to the king who had his own secrets he didn't think anyone knew. Within the next few months, King Magnuz would be dead. The transplants to replace the organs torn apart by the assassin's bullets hadn't worked. The clock ticked down for them all. If losing her father once had been devastating for Elle, what would it be like to lose him twice, and *after* she found out he'd never reached out to her in the ten years she'd been on her own? Telling her the truth wouldn't give her father any more time, and the end result would be the same.

"Nothing." The lie left a foul taste in his mouth, one he wasn't sure he'd ever stop tasting.

She narrowed her eyes and gave him a look that seemed to dig into the darkest parts of his soul and find him lacking. "Really, it doesn't seem like nothing."

"Every man has secrets." He put a lightness into his tone he didn't feel. He had to maneuver away from this topic. He got off his stool and rounded the island to her side. "Anyway..." Nudging a strand of hair away from her ear, he inhaled the sultry scent that drove him to distraction. "It's *Roman Holiday* rules, remember?"

Cupping her chin, he turned her so she faced him and went in for a kiss. Whisper soft and harshly demanding, it was meant to distract them both from the dark turn their conversation had taken and the even darker things left unsaid. She opened for him, and he slid his tongue inside, teasing her and tormenting himself until she pushed him away.

"That won't work forever, you know," she said, more than a little bit breathless, color brightening her cheeks.

"What's that?" he asked, letting his hands travel over her hips and up under the hem of his shirt she was wearing.

"Kissing me to shut me up." She stepped out of his grasp.

Fingers still tingling from touching her, he took a deep breath to regain some sanity before he threw her over his shoulder caveman style and carried her back up to his bed. "Sounds like it's already wearing off."

She dragged her fingers through her long hair and swallowed hard. "Look, I understand the why of what you did, I do, but it still hurts. I was so scared and alone in the beginning. That passed and I got my footing, what I thought was a deserved scholarship, a rent-controlled apartment, and a snarky old lady neighbor who made me laugh even when I had a fever and a nose that wouldn't stop running. I stopped being scared, but I was never not alone."

"I'm sorry." It took everything he had not to rush over to her and tell her she'd never be alone again, that she'd always have him, but another lie was the last thing she needed right now. "We did the best we could."

"You did. And so did I." A decisive nod—the future queen was back. "Are you responsible for the job at Dylan's?"

"We may have gotten your résumé moved to the top of the pile, but you earned it on your own."

"And if the threat from the Fjende hadn't appeared, would you have kept watching from a distance?"

"Yes." He was beginning to hate that fucking word.

She considered him with a distant, calculating look, her earlier open vulnerability stored away somewhere he couldn't touch. He wasn't surprised; she'd had years of practice of hiding her true self. So which one was the true Elle? The woman who melted under his touch, the spitfire who challenged his every move, the engaging stylist who teased and flirted, or the future queen as icy as she was fiery? Then, in one of those flash-of-realization moments that seem shouted down from heaven, Dom realized he didn't care, because he wanted them all. He wanted her for more than a *Roman Holiday* escape, and he couldn't have her. His mission and her duty took precedence over his heart.

"I'm going to go shower." She turned and started for the door.

"Elle." The five feet between them felt like miles. "Are we good?"

She stilled but didn't turn to look back. "I don't know."

And then she was gone.

He wanted to chase after her, kiss her until she couldn't remember her name, let alone all he'd revealed, but she needed space and time to digest the conversation. So Dom forced himself to sit back down on the bar stool at the island and drink the last of his coffee while he watched the clock's second hand tick forward.

Chapter Eleven

After discovering even a thirty-minute super-hot shower wouldn't drain the chalet's hot water tank or get rid of the disappointment clinging to her heart, Elle squeezed the heavy wet out of her hair and stepped out of the shower. Steam covered the large mirror over the double sinks and hung heavy in the air.

She understood Dom's reasoning for not coming for her until he didn't have a choice, but that didn't alleviate the hurt. Ten years was a long time to think that you were alone in the world. Then she'd met Dom, and despite everything that should have sent her running, it was like she was finally with her people—the ones who understood without her having to explain a thing.

Then he'd dropped his little bombshell and cracked the foundation of whatever was building between them...and there *was* something. She knew it the same way she knew her pulse was going to skyrocket when he walked into a room, the way in their training matches she knew he would take off the kid gloves because too much was at risk to pussyfoot around, and the way her soul settled any time he was near. He might not be her people, but he could be her person. Another time, another place...she would have run like the wind to get away from the feelings he caused, but their limited time together had one advantage. She didn't have to worry about losing him, because she'd never really have him no matter how much she realized she wanted to. All she had was the next thirty hours. The question, was how did she want to spend them? With Dom, pretending there wasn't a jet to Elskov waiting for them at the end of it all.

Wrapping the thick white towel around her, she walked out of the bathroom into the massive guest room and stopped dead in her tracks. Dom sat on the end of her bed, the shirt of his she'd worn down to breakfast twisted in his hands. God, he looked delicious. Contrite, proud, and unbroken all in one tall, muscled, Viking warrior package here to accept whatever she wanted to dish out at him, because he could take it. He'd thrown on pants and a dark blue button-up shirt. There wasn't a wrinkle to be seen beyond the crumpled mass of white fabric crushed in his large hands.

"I was beginning to wonder if you'd drowned in there." He tossed the shirt to the side and leaned against the carved walnut post at the end of the bed like he had every right to be there.

It was a shock to realize that for the first time, the image of a man in her personal space didn't freak her out. It was right where she wanted him. No. She wanted him in it. Naked. Sweaty. Hard. She stalked across the room, stopping between his wide-spread thighs. "Showers help me clear my head."

"So what did you decide?"

Toying with the tiny buttons on his shirt, she slipped one and then another free. "We're okay."

Torment clearly written on his face, he grabbed her wrist and forced her arm back to her side before releasing her as if he couldn't trust himself to touch her at that moment. "Not that I should ask this, but why?"

And wasn't the fact that he asked the hard questions one of the things she loved most about him... Loved? *Yes.* The answer smoothed all of her ragged edges.

"Neither of us was in an enviable situation. We both did the best we could." She raised her fingers to the corner of the towel tucked between her breasts, releasing it and letting the towel drop. "Any more questions?"

"Not a damn one." He started in on the rest of his shirt buttons.

"Good." She shoved his shoulders so he flopped back onto her bed hard enough that the inky-blue decorative pillows went flying. "Then let's get on with this holiday."

Crawling up his body, she glided her cheek over his hard thighs and the even harder cock pushing against his pant leg before sitting up with a little extra drama and throwing her head back so the damp strands of her hair slapped against her bare back. Judging by the dark, hungry look he aimed at her stiff nipples, Dom obviously liked the show and how it had made her breasts jiggle. Ignoring the temptation to dangle her breasts in his face and let him have a lick, she straddled his hips and knocked away his hands from the buttons on his shirt. Giving him a sassy wink, she set to work stripping him bare.

"Oh, you think you're in charge?" He stretched and rested his hands behind his head, amusement curling his lips into a smirk.

"I know I am." And he was about to find out exactly what that meant.

In a flash, his palms were on her hips, his fingers curled into her flesh, sending a delicious shiver through her. "I could have you on your back and spread wide for me in two seconds."

"My bed"—she peeled off one of his hands from her flesh—"my rules." The other came up without a fight, and she leaned forward, making sure to let her nipples come tantalizingly close to his lips, and placed his hands above his head.

"What are those?" he asked.

The vein in his temple went into overdrive, but he kept his hands where she put them, watching her close as she sat, this time farther down on his thighs.

Dropping her hands to his pants' top button, she dragged her teeth across her bottom lip and gave him a cocky wink as the button popped free. "You sit back, and I do everything I can to make you lose control."

He tensed underneath her. "I don't lose control."

"You've never been in my bed before." She cupped him through the thin material that did little to lessen the effect touching his dick had on both of them.

"Okay, then." He let out a half moan, half sigh, and let his eyes close. "Let's see what you've got."

She pulled down his zipper and slid her hand inside so she could wrap her fingers around the velvety heat of his cock. One, two, three slow strokes in the tight confines of his pants and Dom's jaw had tightened, his hands fists against the fluffy white pillows.

"Lift your hips," she demanded, her own lust turning her voice husky.

He did, and she yanked his pants down over his round ass, tree trunk–strong thighs, and over the rest of the blond hair–covered legs. After tossing the pants aside, she began to work her way back up his legs, slow and easy with light touches and the barest of kisses on his inner thighs until she met the base of his standing cock. She wrapped her hand around him again, and he twitched under her touch, the head swollen and wet. Keeping her tongue flat, she licked her way up the shaft to the top, sucking him in and tasting the salty proof of his desire.

His ass tightened, and he moaned, but he didn't thrust into her mouth, filling her like she wanted—and she wanted all of him. So she took him. Deep. Using her lips, her tongue, and her hands on his balls, she took him in until she didn't think she could anymore.

"Fuck, Elle, that is so good." His praise came out harsh and strained, right on the edge of losing control.

Right where she wanted him. Relenting, she released him and started slow and steady strokes as her other hand worked the base, twisting with enough pressure to make him gasp with pleasure. Looking up, she found his eyes were no longer closed. He watched her as she lavished the kind of attention on his dick that he'd given her earlier.

Keeping her gaze locked on him, she moved her hands to his lean hips, tracing her nails across the taut muscles of his ass, and then lowered her mouth inch by glorious inch until she took all of him in her mouth and began to slide back until only the tip remained. She gave it a soft suck, and that's when he broke. A groan tore from his mouth, and his hands were buried in her hair, tangling in the damp strands, as he thrust up. Digging her nails into his ass, she held on as his hips rose and fell in time with the up and down strokes of her mouth. Again and again and again she slid him between her wet lips until he finally lost his battle with control and released it all with an orgasm that left him panting and her licking the last of him from her lips like a cat enjoying the last drops of cream.

Still catching his breath, he peeked at her through half-open eyes. "You look way too happy with yourself."

That satisfied growl disguised as a smart-ass remark did things to her insides. She wasn't sure if she should be glad he'd come into her life, if only for such a short time, or if she should be wishing he'd never kidnapped her from Dylan's in the first place.

"Are you saying I need to work on my technique?" She

gave his still half-hard cock a light stroke, confident her skills were top-notch and he knew it.

"No." He locked his legs around her hips and tumbled her onto her back. "I'm saying now it's my turn."

. . .

Looking down at her, her cheeks flushed with anticipation and her bare tits rising and falling with each fast breath, Dom forgot his name for a second.

"What's wrong?" she asked as she trailed her fingers through the deep valley between her tits. "Did you forget what comes next?"

There it was, the challenge he hadn't realized he'd grown to crave from her.

"You've got some mouth on you." That tasted of home and the future and infinite possibilities.

"I seem to recall you like that part of me," she said and blew a kiss at him.

Beauty, brains, and a sharp tongue. She was fucking fantastic. How easy would it be to fall in love with her? Not that he could. Not that he would. But for tonight he could pretend that it was just them. No queen. No billionaire. No country on the edge. Just two people who had one night left before her jet took off at seven p.m. tomorrow. He wasn't going to be with Elle then, but he sure as hell was with her now, and he was going to make it count.

She reached up and cupped his face in her small hands, all the teasing flirtation that had lit up her face before replaced by concern digging lines across her forehead. "What is it?"

"You're amazing." And it was the most truthful thing he'd ever told her.

"Why, sir," she said in a fake southern accent that couldn't cover the worry in her voice. "You're going to make me blush."

"No. Really. It's enough to make me wish…" What, that she wasn't Princess Eloise? That their lives wouldn't separate for good as soon as she got on that jet? That the one goal he'd had for most of his adult life would fall to the wayside so he could be with her? That he could kidnap her again, only this time to be queen of nothing more than his private island in the Caribbean?

The creases in her forehead smoothed, and her lips curled into a bittersweet smile. "Yeah, me too."

He stared at her, searching for words…for an explanation…for understanding, but he wasn't equipped for this, for falling in love with Elle. So he said with actions what he couldn't get out in words.

The kiss was gentle, a brush of his lips against hers, and he poured everything he had into the soft exploration of her mouth. She opened beneath him, and he slipped his tongue inside, every part of him focused on taking her higher. He caressed her silky smooth skin, gliding his palms over her, memorizing her every curve. The gentle slope of her tits topped by blush-colored nipples that grew harder under his touch as he rolled them between his fingers, tugging just hard enough to make her sigh into the kiss.

It was a sound, so needy and wanting, that broke him all over again, and like before Dom let go of the control that gave him some emotional distance from Elle. He tore his mouth from hers, tracing kisses across her jaw and down the column of her throat.

"Dom, I need you."

"What do you need, sweetheart?" He sucked one of her puckered nipples into his mouth, relishing her desire and desperate moan, and skimmed his palm over her stomach.

She lifted her hips in response. "You inside me."

"I can give you this." He slid one finger and then a second between her slick folds.

Her eyes squeezed shut; she undulated against him. "That feels so good."

Keeping his strokes shallow, he teased her, drawing out the pleasure. "You're so tight for me."

"For you. Always for you."

"That's right." He added his thumb to the mix, swirling it around her clit as he curled his fingers inside her to rub against the bundle of nerves inside her entrance. "For me."

She reached up, holding onto his shoulders as if she was afraid he'd go before she got where she needed to go. "Don't stop."

"Never."

Her eyes snapped open at the promise he couldn't keep. At that moment he saw it all in her eyes' depths. The hope. The fear. The yearning. She knew, just like he did, that this moment was fleeting. Like the fog across the grasslands in Elskov, it would dissipate, leaving only memories and the endless wondering about what could have been. And if he didn't love her already, that epiphany would have sealed it for him. Even though he couldn't keep her, she was his, just as he was hers.

"I know," he whispered, not trusting himself to say it louder. "I know."

Her fingers dug into his shoulders as he stroked her, increasing his speed in time with her moans and the rise of her hips as she ground against his palm, faster and harder, until her body went rigid underneath him and she climaxed.

"Dom," she sighed, a satisfied smile curling her lips as she pulled his face down to hers and kissed him with enough passion to knock him kneeless.

Pulling away, intent on finding his pants and the condom in his wallet, he turned to the end of the bed.

"Don't do it," she said.

For a heartbeat he thought she meant she wanted him to take her away from Elskov and everything waiting for her there. He whipped his head around to face her and saw nothing but lust and steely determination.

"I'm on the pill. I'm clean. I want to feel you."

God, could he take it? "Are you sure?"

"Without a doubt. Right now you're mine, and I'm yours." She crooked a finger at him. "Come back here."

Shoving aside everything else but the here and now, he did. Sliding his body over hers, he lined himself up with her entrance and then plunged inside with one long thrust. This was what he wanted. No barriers. No lies of omission. Just them, with nothing in between. The pleasure was overwhelming.

"You feel so fucking good," he managed to get out, trying to give her time to adjust to him.

"I think that's my line." She raised her hips, taking him deeper until he was buried to the hilt.

It was too much and not nearly enough. He couldn't hold back anymore. Thrusting inside her and withdrawing with increasing fury, he lost himself in her. Again and again, he plunged forward and retreated to the sound of her mewls of pleasure that only made his balls tighten as he neared the point of no return.

"Elle, I can't hold off much—"

"Come inside me, Dom," she demanded. "I want to feel you spill into me."

It only took one more stroke for him to bury himself balls deep in her warmth before he did, his orgasm crashing through him like a tsunami, washing away everything but Elle.

Rolling to the side before he collapsed on top of her, he wrapped his arms around her and pulled her close. Neither of them said anything as they snuggled close. No doubt she was trying to make sense of what had just happened as much as he had. Nothing made sense anymore except for Elle, and that scared him more than any threat from the Fjende possibly could.

Chapter Twelve

Three hours later according to the digital clock, Elle stretched out in the empty bed and wished she could make time stop. Dom's phone had rung a few minutes ago, and he'd apologized before taking the call in the library on the other side of that crazy *Scooby-Doo* hidden door. No doubt more business—that she'd have to pry out of him—about how to get her into the Kronig without tipping off the Fjende. The man was damned frustrating with how under wraps he kept every bit of planning.

Still naked as she'd been when she'd had the best sex of her life a few hours ago—so good the glow of it clung to her skin—she got out of bed as quietly as possible and crept across the bedroom to the hidden door. It wasn't closed all the way, letting through the conversation the other side. Straining to hear, she leaned close to the opening.

"She needs to know about you, sir." Dom's voice carried through the midafternoon quiet blanketing the chalet.

Since she was the only woman she'd seen at the chalet, Elle knew Dom had to be talking about her. She nudged the door open a few inches, thankful the well-oiled hinges didn't make a sound.

"I understand your concerns, but I respectfully submit that your reasoning is faulty. She's not the girl you knew anymore. She's a strong, smart, practically fearless woman who will lead Elskov because she's chosen to, not because of your cat and mouse games."

Cat and mouse games? What the hell?

"King Magnuz, she *is* your daughter, and she deserves to know you're alive."

Whatever came after was drowned out in the white noise filling her head. Her father was alive. Her father. Was. Alive. And Dom knew. Judging by the familiarity with which he'd spoken with her father, he'd known the whole time. He'd said he wasn't the Resistance's leader, so that left one man who could be. Her father.

"I realize that, Your Highness, but it doesn't change the facts," Dom said, his tone icy. "If you don't tell her, I will."

"Too late." She choked out the declaration through a throat tight with emotion. "She already knows."

Dom whipped around, a red flush creeping across his face. Guilt? Remorse? Embarrassment? It didn't matter. The kidnapping, the watching her from afar—she could understand that coming from a man who'd never known her and who was focused solely on the goal of taking back Elskov. But her own father? No. Strangely, Dom's betrayal about her father being alive hurt just as much, if not more.

"Sir, she's here. Would you like to—" His mouth formed a straight line and he disconnected the call. "Must have been cut off."

"Really?" She snorted, emptiness settling in her belly, freezing all the fiery anger that no doubt would come later. "Sounded to me like he hung up on you."

He took a step toward her, dressed only in the slacks he'd

worn earlier and the desperate look of a man who'd fucked up but was going to give fixing things the old college try. "Elle—"

She held up her hand, warding him off. "Don't bother. It doesn't matter."

"Yes, it does." Dom closed the distance between them, stopping only when her palm pressed against his chest.

Touching him burned her, defrosted some of the coldness keeping her sane, but she fought against it. She'd been here before, on her own.

"Wrong," she said, surprised at the hollow sound of her voice. "Does it change what I have to do next?"

"No." He put his hand over hers, holding it tight enough that she could feel the unsteady *thump-thump-thumpity-thump* of his heartbeat.

"Because he's not coming back to Elskov, is he?" She slid her hand free, doing her best to ignore her body's protest at the removal of his heat.

"No."

And there it was. It always came back to that. The goal for him, for her father, for the Resistance, had always been to get her back on the throne whether she wanted to be there or not. But her father had loved Elskov. She'd thought he'd given his life for it. It didn't make sense for him to stay away now when they were so close to taking back the country from the Fjende…unless…her gut clenched.

"What's wrong with him?"

The vein in Dom's temple throbbed, and his jaw went rigid.

"Dammit, tell me!" Her shout exploded in the small space between them.

He sighed and looked away. When he returned his gaze to her face, there was only sympathy shining in his cool blue eyes. "The injuries from the attack—there were…complications. His body is rejecting the transplants one by one. The doctors don't expect him to recover."

It took all the strength she had not to give in to the shock and slide down the wall into a pool of goop at the news. She was mad enough to scream at him for days, but he was her father. Even now, even after everything, she loved him.

"How much time did they give him?"

"A matter of months." He reached for her, but she brushed off his touch.

Understanding jolted her, connecting all of the events of the past week. "That's why you came for me, isn't it?" She lashed out, her anger finally spouting through her frozen core. "Not because of some outside threat, but because you needed a head of state to overthrow that farce of a government and my father couldn't do it."

"The Fjende is out there," Dom snarled back. "They were looking for you." He slammed his palm against the bookshelf door. "They *did* find you."

"Why should I believe you?"

"Because you know I'm telling the truth."

The laugh that spilled out of her was anything but joyful. "Just like I knew my father was dead? Just like I knew I was alone in the world? Just like I knew that someone would be waiting for me when my plane landed in America after the coup?"

"It's not like that." He blanched and looked deflated and so unlike the ultra-confident man he'd always been. "Not between us."

"Funny, that's what I thought, too." She took a step back and brought her hand to the hidden door, ready to swing it shut. "Turns out I was wrong."

"Where are you going?"

He probably thought she was running away, planning to start all over again with a new name and a new life. She'd done it before, she could do it again, but she wasn't going to.

"To pack." Her voice sounded so much steadier than she felt. "Unlike some people, I keep my word. I said I'd return to Elskov and knock the Fjende and their puppet off the throne, and I will."

"We need to bring you up to speed on the details of what will happen at the Kronig."

God, she couldn't. Not with him. She wasn't sure she'd make it another thirty seconds without breaking down. "I'm sure Major Bendtsen can do that. He does know the plan, or is that something you're keeping to yourself?"

He stiffened, and a mask slid into place over his expressive features. Her Viking was gone. She didn't know the man in his place. "I can fill him in, Your Highness."

"Good." She dipped her chin, barely managing to keep her bottom lip from trembling. "Then there's no further reason for us to see each other again."

She spun on the ball of her foot, head held high, and swung the hidden door shut, or at least tried to. Dom's hand on the bookshelf stopped it.

"Elle." Her name was a twisty bit of agony coming from him. "I'm so sorry."

Pain clamped down on her chest, pinching her lungs and squeezing her heart. "Good-bye, Dom."

His hand dropped to his side, and she closed the *Scooby-Doo* door. The ridiculousness of it gave rise to nearly hysterical giggles that she smothered down with the will of a woman who'd been emotionally eviscerated by the two men she'd ever loved.

• • •

Dom stalked through the greenhouse, the thick humidity natural in the glassed-in environment barely registering as he fought with the guilt and the frustration threatening to drag him down. He stopped at the indoor water feature that emptied into a koi pond and shoved the gnome's red hat down with more force than necessary. The trickling water took a different path, revealing the door hiding behind it. Stepping through, he found Major Bendtsen at his usual post monitoring the wall of video screens showing the chalet and grounds from multiple angles.

"What time is your replacement scheduled to come on?"

The major kept his eyes on the screens. "Twenty minutes, sir."

"Good. That gives us enough time for me to brief you on the plans once we arrive in Elskov."

Now that got the other man's attention. The major turned, his eyes wide. "I thought you wanted to hold off on that until right before the jet takes off."

That had been the plan, to sit down with Elle and the major to outline exactly what would happen from the time their private jet touched down. He'd spent weeks thinking up every angle and circumventing every hurdle the Fjende would have in place. The Kronig was what he'd been working toward his whole life, but somehow it had become even more important to him that every move be controlled so that Elle would be kept as safe as possible. Right now, that was all that mattered to him.

"I need you to share the plan with Princess Eloise and ensure all of her questions and concerns are addressed."

Bendtsen's eyes got even wider before the normally taciturn major turned his attention back to the screens. "I see." His eyes narrowed as he looked closer at the monitor showing the north gate.

Dom's gaze went to the blank screen that normally would have shown Elle's room. One quick flick of the switch and he could see her, watch her, pretend the last time he'd see her wasn't going to be in a few hours. Even as mad as she was at him, she wasn't half as mad as he was at himself. He shouldn't have lied to her about her father. He knew how awful it was to lose a parent—hell, he'd lost both. If he were to find out tomorrow they were still alive and had hidden that from him, he'd go nuclear.

His hand was up and over the button to turn on the monitor showing Elle's room before he even realized it. Then the light above one of the monitors started blinking, then another and another.

It took effort, but he spotted the men moving through the chalet's grounds. Judging by their formation and weapons, they were highly trained Fjende guards.

"Fuck." He clicked on the emergency comm line that went to the entire security team. "We've been breached. I repeat, we've been breached. Lethal force authorized." Dom disconnected and spun around to face the major. "How the fuck did they get this far inside the line without anyone knowing?"

The other man's fingers moved like lightning on the keyboard, and he brought up two video feeds of the same shot—one live with Fjende thugs exchanging fire with his team, the other showing the same scene minus the firefight.

"They hacked into our system and mirrored the feeds," the major said.

That's when the lights inside the security operations bunker dropped down to low-generator-power mode, signaling that automatic safety measures had been enacted.

Elle!

Dom rushed for the door and tried to yank it open. Nothing happened. Fuck. The security operations room had been designed like a panic room. In the event of a problem, no one got in and no one got out. The monitors still worked, but that didn't make for two-way communication. The white intercom box above the screens caught his eye.

"Tap in to her room intercom, Bendtsen. I need to warn her." Heart ramming against his rib cage, he flipped on her room monitor. She was there. He released the breath he'd been holding captive. Her eyes were wide and she was looking around; knowing her she was on the hunt for a weapon.

"Elle, I need you to get in your closet!" he yelled into the intercom mic. "There's a panic room behind the back wall. Barricade yourself in."

She grabbed a sharp, steel letter opener and slid it into the side of her knee-high boot. "What's going on, Dom?"

"The Fjende. They're here. Get in the panic room." His voice shook as he mentally cursed himself for not being with her. "I will come for you."

"Dom—"

"I will *always* come for you, Elle, but I need you to stick to the plan right now." Closing his eyes for a second, he sent up a quick prayer thanking God she was still okay and begging that she'd stay that way. "And the plan is for you to get into the—"

The sound of shouting and glass breaking blasted through the intercom. The line went dead. He snapped open his eyes. Each monitor showed only white snow. The Fjende had managed to cut communications. There was nothing he could do to save her. No way for him to get to her and protect her. He had no control, not when it really fucking mattered. It was enough to make his hands shake. He hadn't been this scared since his parents had gone missing. They'd ended up mutilated, their bodies dumped in a central square.

He clamped his jaw tight. That wasn't going to happen to Elle.

He yanked out a chair and rolled up his sleeves as he sat down. He hadn't earned his first million as a venture capitalist. No, the kitty money had come from a successful software program he'd created. The eight-inch-thick steel door was controlled by a locking program not linked to the chalet's main power grid or its regular security features. Sometimes being a paranoid control freak paid off, and he was going to make sure this was just such a time.

Lowering his fingers to the keyboard, he let out a deep breath. The Fjende were out there coming after Elle, and the only thing standing between him and saving her was breaking the code to unlock the security headquarters' door. He didn't have time to waste.

. . .

Elle fought to keep from giving in to the blind terror scraping her from the inside out. The men had crashed through the French doors of her balcony. She'd jumped for cover and found a hiding space behind the massive walnut dressing table.

Her gaze darted around the room, counting the number of black-booted men searching through the large bedroom. The closet with its panic room was on the other side of the room. She peeked around the dressing table's corner. No one was near the closet door. Her pulse pounded in her ears, and her hands shook as she gauged the distance.

She had surprise on her side. If she could sprint fast enough, she just might be able to get inside the closet before they knew what was going on. Taking a deep breath, she readied herself for the mad dash of her life. That's when a giant man stepped directly between her and the closet. Looking down, he smiled at her. It wasn't a nice smile.

"Princess Eloise, we've been looking for you for some time," he said. "I am Walther Henriksen, the head of your royal guard. If you'll come with me, we'll have you back in Elskov by morning."

"I'm not going with you."

"You don't have a choice, Your Highness."

"I always have a choice." She settled into her stance, legs shoulder width apart, hands loose.

Walther watched her with amusement, one white-blond

eyebrow raised. "I'm easily a foot taller, have a hundred pounds on you, and am backed up by a small platoon of men who wouldn't hesitate to shoot you in the ass with a tranquilizer if I even look in their direction."

Elle took a slow look around, taking in the blond giant in front of her and the six equally large men dressed in head-to-toe black armed with assault rifles and smaller dart guns. Walther hadn't been joking about the tranquilizers. Her gaze slid to the *Scooby-Doo* door hidden in the bookshelf. She could make it, but could she get through in time?

"I do like that you have such spirit. It will serve you well as queen." He paused and gave her a grin that chilled her soul. "With a little molding, of course."

Getting to the hidden door wasn't an option, and if they got her with a dart gun and knocked her out, she had no hope of escape. One of the first lessons Dom had taught her in their one-on-one training sessions was to always keep as many options as possible open. If she didn't give in to the panic gnawing away at the back of her brain, she could still come out on top.

The Resistance, for all their faults, wouldn't leave her to the Fjende's not-so-tender mercies. Dom never would. He'd find her; she just had to keep her head until then. If nothing else, she lived to fight another day. And she would.

"Fine," she said making her tone as haughty as she could. "Let's go."

"As you command, Your Highness." He led her to the balcony of her room and grabbed her around the waist before hooking himself to a thick nylon rope line. "Don't fight. A drop from this high won't kill you, but you'll be lucky to walk away with a broken leg."

With that tiny bit of warning, he hauled her over the banister, and they zipped down the two floors to the garden below. As soon as she stood, the men in black formed a wall of solid, silent muscle around her and ushered her to the waiting helicopter.

Trepidation settled like cement around her feet with each step closer they got to the navy blue helicopter adorned with her family's royal seal on the doors. She looked left, then right. Barely any sunlight could get through between the guards' close-pressed bodies.

Leaning down to avoid the helicopter blades, Walther swept open the door. "After you, Your Highness."

Anxiety making her skin itch even as she desperately searched for a way out, she crouched and got onto the helicopter. Another huge guard stood outside the door on the opposite side, effectively blocking escape from that route.

She sat down in the seat closest to the door anyway; perhaps she'd have a second to make a move when they landed. Walther took the seat next to her, reached across her lap, and fastened the seat belt tight. A second later the door closed, and then they were aloft. Figuring the best defense right now was to act as royally aloof as plausible, she angled her face away from Walther. The pinprick against her neck told her just how big a mistake that choice was. Liquid fire surged through her system, holding her prisoner to her own body. She couldn't lift her arms. Her legs were useless. Her eyes began to drift shut.

"Oh, no, Princess, no going to sleep just yet. We've got something to show you," Walther yelled into her ear, loud enough she could hear him despite the noise of the helicopter blades chopping through the cold mountain air. "Look down."

He grabbed her chin and turned her so she faced the window. The chalet glimmered in the setting sun as it sat surrounded by mountain peaks as far as she could see. Her foggy brain tried to make sense of why he wanted to her watch, but all that kept going through her head was that Dom was down there. Her Dom. The one who despite how mad she was at him right now was her person, the one she wanted. The one who would come for her, just as she would always come for him.

"Five, four, three," Walther chanted, "two, one."

The chalet exploded into a massive ball of orange fire, the force of which shook the air around the helicopter and jostled her chin loose from Walther's grip. Her head fell forward, landing with a hard thump against her chest, and her body was held upward only by the strength of the seat belt across her waist and shoulders. Dom had been in there. Somewhere. Another explosion rocked the helicopter, knocking her head so her forehead rested against the window and she couldn't turn away from the fire and smoke billowing from the chalet.

Misery squeezed her heart, squashing it until there was nothing left. The last thing she'd told him was good-bye, when even as she'd said it, she'd known it wouldn't have been forever. Not between them. Their lives had come crashing together wish such force that they'd been melded together. No single word was going to sever that.

A third explosion boomed, and the chalet came crumbling down. Dom was down there, somewhere, in the smoking rumble. He wasn't dead. She wouldn't believe that. She couldn't. A silent scream rang in her ears, the mournful keening of loss mixed with the raw fury.

Using every bit of strength that she had, she slid her gaze over to the man whom she'd someday kill slowly and with as much pain as possible. He didn't seem bothered by the hatred he had to see blazing in her eyes.

"And that, Princess, is what we do to those who try to take on the Fjende." Walther laughed and sat back in his seat, closing his eyes like a man without a care in the world.

If she could have moved a single limb, she would have torn him to shreds before shoving him out of the helicopter, even if that meant she plummeted to her death with him. She didn't want to believe Walther. How could anyone have survived the attack? No one could have, not even Dom.

Chapter Thirteen

Dom strained to hear the voice above the static on the backup radio that was their only communication with what was left of the team outside.

"She's not here," Sergeant Christiansen said, the words garbled but the message clear.

The vise on his chest loosened a few turns. "How can you be sure?"

"Thermal scan was negative," Christiansen said. "It confirms the report from Bravo Company, which had visual of a small unit escorting a prisoner to a helicopter."

Reports of the royal jet taking off from a private airport in Harbor City had come in within an hour of the first explosion. Dom didn't believe in coincidence. "We'll operate on the assumption she's on her way to Elskov, but I want that part of the chalet excavated first."

"Copy that, sir," the other man said. "Should I send a secondary team to your area?"

"Negative." He disconnected the line and shoved back from the keyboard.

He'd broken through the mechanism holding the operations room door locked, but it wouldn't do any good now. The metal door whined as the fire blazed on the other side of the chalet's security room. Dom's ears still rang from the explosions that had rocked the chalet to its foundations. The only thing that had saved them was the fact that his paranoia had convinced him to build the security room into the side of the mountain; otherwise, they would be buried under several tons of the stones used to build the chalet. The explosions had been too strong for any other outcome to be possible.

He'd be worried if he'd thought Elle was still here, but the Fjende hadn't come here to kill her. They needed her too much, at least for now. Dom had to get to her before it was too late.

He glanced over at the man who'd been his trusted number two for the past six years. What he was about to ask went so far beyond the call of duty that he couldn't allow the other man to embark on what could very well be a suicide mission without giving him an out.

"Major," he said. "You don't have to come with me, but if you do, it doubles our chances of getting Elle back safely. Are you in?"

The other man grinned. "Are you asking me to help you storm the castle?"

"Shit, Major, you've got a sense of humor. I never would have guessed." Throwing open the door to the small armory built into the side of the security room, Dom grabbed a duffel bag and started stuffing it with guns, ammunition, and peripheral equipment.

Without a word, Major Bendtsen stepped up beside Dom and started doing the same.

Dom finished filling his bag and snagged a set of keys from the top of the rack. The action triggered what looked like a solid wall splitting in the middle and sliding open like elevator doors, revealing another door with a handprint scanner. He held his palm up to the screen. A green light traveled from top to bottom; the scanner beeped twice, and the door swung open. A blast of freezing-cold air swept into the room.

Lights clicked on one after the other, revealing a long tunnel carved into the mountain at a steep decline. When he'd commissioned the backup plan to his backup plan, this had been the escape route to get the king or Elle off the mountain and miles away from the chalet, into a sports utility vehicle and to the private airstrip where the jet bound for Elskov was waiting for them; they'd be there by morning. The Kronig would only be hours away, but the early prep team was already there waiting for his arrival. The king had been on his way from Madrid when the Fjende had hit the chalet.

What he hadn't considered until it was too late was what would happen if the security protocols worked as planned, except he was trapped inside and Elle was left to fend for herself against the Fjende. He'd fucked up, but that wasn't going to happen again. No matter what it took, he was going to make sure Elle was safe.

After that? He'd walk away from the woman he loved, knowing it was the best thing for her. She had a duty to her country. She'd made a promise to accept the crown, and she'd stick to it. Princesses didn't marry common foreigners, no matter how rich or loyal. He'd bow, and like the reporter in *Roman Holiday*, he'd walk away. Then he'd get drunk enough to forget the way she tasted and the sassy challenge every time she opened her sweet mouth and the way she could knock him sideways with just a look.

• • •

Elle stretched her fingers. It wasn't much, but it was more than she'd been able to do when Walther and his thug patrol had hauled her onto the private jet and buckled her into a leather seat embossed with the royal crest. Her attempts to catch the eye of the flight attendant for help during the fourteen-hour flight to Elskov had been futile. No doubt she'd been chosen with the same evil care as Walther's armed minions.

They taxied across the deserted private airport. It wouldn't do for the press to find out she'd been dragged home like a drugged-up sheep. Instead, they'd circled a small, local airport before descending to the asphalt runway. The wheels touched down, and she bounced in her seat, watching the countryside rush by as the jet slowed to a stop near the utilitarian terminal.

She wasn't supposed to be here, not yet—that hadn't been Dom's plan. He would be so pissed if he'd known how screwed up his plan had become. The image of him with that cocky grin and the Viking swagger gave way to the remembered sound of explosions and the heat whipping up from the ground so intense she'd felt it lick against her skin even in the helicopter. Tears pricked her eyes as she blinked them away, grinding her teeth together in an effort to keep from letting the cry rip from her throat.

All of her emotions mixed up to form a sticky ball of hurt, regret, and betrayal that made even breathing difficult. How could she be so mad at Dom and so heartbroken at the same time? It didn't make sense…but one thing did. She looked over at Walther across from her. The bastards would pay for killing him. She'd see to it if it were the last thing she ever did.

The FASTEN SEAT BELT sign overhead dinged off.

"Welcome home, Your Highness." Walther unsnapped his seat belt and leaned forward to undo hers. "I hope you had a pleasant flight."

She flipped him off, surprising herself that she could. The drugs were wearing off fast now. Good, something in her favor.

He chuckled, but his left eye twitched enough to add some menace to the soft sound. "That rude nonverbal gesture is not fitting with your station, but that won't matter after the Kronig."

She worked to get her dry mouth to cooperate. "What happens then?"

Information was power, and she needed all she could get right now. The letter opener tucked into her boot scratched her calf, but she celebrated the pain after hours of numbness.

"That's up to you." Walther shrugged. "Your cousin Alton will be giving you the details, but the choice comes down to a wedding or a painful—agonizing, really—daily life. I'll let you wonder which one he's hoping you'll choose."

That wasn't going to happen. She hadn't been in the castle for a decade, but she'd grown up there. She knew every side passage, every unused tunnel, and a million shortcuts. All she needed was a few minutes to herself and she'd be outside the walls before Walther here had any idea. Of course, what she'd do after she had no clue. Elskov was an island, and she could only run so far, but she'd figure that out once she made it to the coast. An old memory tickled her brain. Alton's family had a home outside Faroe City, a huge monstrosity of a place on the coast with several small boats and a yacht. If he wasn't in residence, she could get there. It had been years, but every Elskovian child learned how to pilot a boat at a young age, even the country's princess. She could be in Denmark thirteen hours after setting off. Once there, she'd announce the princess was alive and do whatever it took to push the Fjende out of Elskov. But first she needed intel. "Where is my dear cousin?"

Walther gave a bored sigh and checked his watch. "Waiting for you at the castle."

It was obvious he could care less. The lightbulb went off. "You're not just the royal guard, you're leading the Fjende."

He stood, a smirk curling his thin lips, and took a deep bow. "At your service, Your Highness."

Icy certainty froze her to the spot; she couldn't wait to wipe that shitty look off his face with the tip of a sharp knife. "I'm going to enjoy killing you."

"Funny." Something dark and deadly snapped in his navy blue eyes. "That's exactly what I told your father before I pulled the trigger."

"You bastard." She bolted from her seat, ready to take him out with a quick jab to the esophagus followed by a knee to the nuts, but her legs gave way as soon as she was upright. She fell into a heap on her chair, the contents of her stomach roiling.

"No, actually, I'm not," he sneered. "My parents are still married and delightfully unaware that it's our family who should be on the Elskov throne, but your lot dabbled in poison and voilà, the Dahl dynasty ended during a single dinner. One quick-witted Madsen took advantage of the power vacuum, and your ancestors stole the throne. I've just taken it back."

"How is that even possible if all of the Dahls died?"

"Now you of all people should know that while it's not easy, royalty can hide among the commoners. A new last name, a hiding of the evidence, and you're all set. Of course, what my parents believe only to be an old family legend is in actuality truth. We are the lost Dahls, and the throne is ours; it is divine provenance," he said, his voice ringing with conviction as a calmness settled over him.

Walther wasn't crazy. He wasn't greedy. He was a true believer. Bile rose in Elle's throat. The urge to run as far away as fast as possible seized her by the throat. If she couldn't find a way to escape, she'd forfeit her life. She jiggled her legs; they felt better. Maybe not 100 percent, but close. If she could piss him off just enough to get him to really go on a rant, she could make a break for it.

"Wow," she said with just enough of the insolence she used to impress the snotty, spoiled, rich teenagers who came to Dylan's showroom floor. "It must really gall you then to see my cousin Alton on it."

The air sizzled around Walther. "He won't be there for much longer. Whether you marry him or not, you will carry my heir, and a true-blood Dahl will inherit the throne, righting a wrong made hundreds of years ago."

Her stomach lurched, and her mouth tasted of foulness. "It's not going to happen," she said, her voice trembling. "I'm not alone anymore."

"Did you miss the"—he raised one finger, then a second, and then a final finger—"three explosions when we took off? There's nothing left of your Resistance."

She pictured Dom, his wide smile and broad shoulders as they sparred in the training room. The warmth of him as they'd snuggled watching *Roman Holiday*. The feel of his hands on her bare flesh. The look in his eyes when he'd come with her name on his lips.

Had it been love? Yes.

Dom had deserved more out of life than to die in her name. Grief twisted her heart until all that was left was fury and regret.

Walther reached into the pocket of his wool coat. He withdrew a needle and uncapped it. "So do I need to shoot you up again, or can I count on you to be a good little princess who will walk across the tarmac to the waiting car and not make a fuss?"

Clear liquid formed a drop that clung to the end of the needle. It had taken her fourteen hours to get back after he'd shot her up last time. There was no way she was going back under. She'd buy her time. He couldn't have his eyes on her with the needle at the ready all of the time.

"Elskov is an island," she said. "Where in the world would

I go if I did manage to get away?"

"That is the smartest thing I've heard you say since you woke up." He yanked a thick metal cuff from his other coat pocket and clapped it around her wrist, securing it in place with a thin chain. "Now this will ensure you stay with us. Part GPS tracker and part ticking time bomb, it will let us know where you are at all times, and if you try to take it off, this little bit here"—he pointed to what looked like a small diamond—"opens up and releases the same numbing agent you just enjoyed, but in a much more powerful dose. You'll be on the ground before your head even processes what happened. Honestly, I'm not sure if I'd prefer the sure thing of knowing where you are or the fun of seeing you fight the toxin." He held out his arm. "Now, shall we?"

It went against every instinct she had, but Elle slid her hand into the crook of his arm and they walked down the jet's staircase. He wanted to take her to the castle? Good. No one knew it better than her. Once she figured out how to remove the damned cuff, she'd slip through Walther's grasp like water.

Her foot had barely touched the tarmac when a blast of wind hit her, carrying the scent of salt water, old memories, and home. It wasn't until that moment that she realized Dom had carried the scent as well. He hadn't, not really. It would have been impossible to bottle Elskov's scent, but somehow he'd smelled like home to her. Even though Dom hadn't made it here with her, he'd brought her home all the same, and she'd do whatever it took to make sure Walther paid dearly for killing the man she loved.

Elle looked through the car's windshield and caught her breath. The castle loomed ahead of them as the car passed through the ancient iron gates. The dark, almost ebony-colored stone castle stood in stark contrast to the cheery blue sky, each of the four turrets reaching upward as if the flagpole atop each could pierce the heavens. Her chest tightened at the sight, and the rush of unexpected tears made the tip of her nose tingle.

She'd grown up playing inside the castle's walls, sneaking into the throne room, pestering the cooks in the kitchen for extra blueberry scones, and hiding among the topiaries in her father's favorite garden. God, she hadn't realized how much she'd missed it. She'd fought against it, but she couldn't deny that Elskov was woven into her DNA.

She was done running.

She was done hiding.

She was home.

Walther's hard grip on her upper arm jolted her out of the bittersweet epiphany.

"Speak a single word once we're inside, and I'll make sure to leave the bruises where they won't show but will hurt the most," he said in a harsh whisper moments before the car pulled to a stop at the private, royal family entrance to the castle.

"Why, Walther." Her smile was as fake as the sweetness in her voice. "You make it sound as if your hold on power isn't as tight as you'd like the world to believe."

He released her arm and grabbed her hair, winding it around his fist and yanking hard. "You better watch your mouth unless you want to end up like your father sooner rather than later."

Retreat was the smart move, but even the idea grated against her skin. Her muscles tensed, wound up with barely repressed fury ready to be unleashed on the man who'd killed Dom and had very nearly done the same to her father. Tearing away layers of his skin with her nails would feel so good. She twisted in her seat enough to improve her angle as much as possible with the death grip Walther had on her hair.

Then the memory of Dom in the training room flashed in her head. *Timing is everything. Don't make a move just because you want to. Wait for your opening and then hold nothing back.*

"Understood." She was so keyed up from the adrenaline rushing through her system, the single word was all she could trust herself with.

He tugged her hair, forcing her head at a painful angle. "Just like that, the little viper puts away her fangs?"

Before she could come up with a plausible lie, the door on Walther's side opened. He shot her another evil glare before letting her hair fall from his tight grip. He got out of the limousine without another word, obviously expecting her to follow. He stopped next to a pair of hulking men who looked like they shopped for suits at the same store as the Harbor City Giant football team's defensive line. As soon as she stepped outside of the car, the duo flanked her. Neither even glanced her way.

"This is your security team," Walther said. "Everywhere you go, they go. Right now you are late for your makeover. A team is waiting for you in your quarters to get rid of that awful hair color, those colored contacts, and your hideous clothing so you once again look like the Her Royal Highness Princess Eloise." He glanced down at the deadly cuff on her wrist. "Don't think I'm fooled by your little act back there in the car. Go ahead and run. I dare you." He gave a curt nod to the guards on either side of her, turned, and strode away.

Elle watched him go, knowing it wouldn't be the last time she'd see him. With any luck, the next time would be when he was begging for his life.

Chapter Fourteen

The sun had yet to turn the sky above Elskov from dawn's pink and orange to bright blue when the jet touched down on an overgrown landing strip outside the capital. Dom had his seat belt undone before the plane finished hitting every one of the potholes on the unused tarmac. A single minute longer than absolutely necessary was too long for Elle to be in the Fjende's hands. He didn't have time to wait for the damn SEAT BELT sign to flicker off. He needed to get to her now.

Major Bendtsen hung up his cell phone. "Our onsite operatives confirm the landing zone is clear."

Good news, but it didn't matter. He'd plow through a thousand Fjende to get to Elle. "The princess?"

"One of our undercovers in the castle has had visual contact," the major said. "She says the princess is unharmed but being watched by two guards at all times."

The jet jerked to a stop, and Dom bounded out of this seat, grabbed his duffel, and rushed to the door. Unwilling to wait for the flight attendant, he threw it open. The stairs unfolded automatically, and he was halfway down before he realized not one but two black sedans were parked along the west edge of the asphalt near where the jet had stopped.

The driver got out of the first sedan and opened the back passenger door. The first thing to emerge was the end of a wooden walking stick, emblazoned with the royal crest on its handle. A frail old man stepped out.

Dom sucked in a surprised gasp. Death clung to the king like dew on a fresh blade of grass. Painfully thin with dark circles under his blue eyes and gray-tinted skin, King Magnuz leaned heavily against his cane. Even his most trusted advisers from the days before the coup wouldn't have recognized him. The driver/bodyguard didn't offer his arm but positioned himself so he could reach out if His Highness needed help.

Shoving away his shock at the king's transformation since he'd seen him a year ago, Dom strode down the stairs and executed a low bow. "Your Highness."

The king motioned for Dom to straighten up. "You're confident your plan will work?"

"Depends on your daughter's willingness to play along." Dom rubbed the back of his neck, unable to shake the feeling that no matter how many backup plans he had, when it came to Elle, surprises were a given. "We'll need her to stay in place until the Kronig begins. Our agent inside the castle is getting a message to the princess when he delivers her breakfast this morning."

"She's a real spitfire—reminds me of her mother." The king let out a weary chuckle tinged with regret and seemed to age another decade in a minute. "She'll never forgive me."

"Why did you want it this way?" The question was out before Dom could stop it. One did not make eye contact with the sovereign, let alone ask invasive question.

"In the beginning, it was because I really did think she was safest on her own with some guardian angels." King Magnuz shrugged, obviously not caring about the break in royal protocol. "Then later I was afraid that if I did see her again, I wouldn't be able to walk away. By then I already knew I was dying. There wasn't a future for us, and it seemed she'd made peace with her new life. Who was I to take that away from her? I'm already her past. She needs to concentrate on Elskov and her future."

"You think it was the right call?" Elle sure as hell hadn't thought so, and Dom agreed with her. If it was the last thing he did, he'd find a way to make up for not telling her about her father.

"That is none of your concern." The king looked up at him, a cool, imperial mask sliding into place over the pain etched into a father's face. "What is, however, is ensuring my daughter's safety. Do you think you can manage it this time?"

There wasn't a doubt in his mind. "Yes, sir."

"Good." The king pivoted slowly toward the open car door, reaching out for his driver/bodyguard's arm to steady himself. "I'll expect an update. I'll be flying out as soon as the Kronig coronation is complete."

Dom started. How could the king go without seeing his daughter—why even bother to show up in the first place? "Why are you here?"

The king got into the backseat but didn't turn toward Dom. Instead, he looked straight ahead, a stubborn tilt to his chin, reminding Dom of Elle every time she'd gotten pissed off at him during the past week.

Finally the king spoke. "You're forgetting your place."

"No, I'm not." Fury on Elle's behalf slapped him across the face, and he fisted his hands to stop from grabbing King Magnuz by the lapels and shaking him. "I'm your daughter's best hope. I'm going to rescue the princess, and once she's safe I'm going to tell her you're here. It'll be her choice to see you one last time or not." He inhaled a deep breath, surprised at his own loss of cool control, and forced a deliberate calm into his voice that he didn't feel. "You're my king, but isn't it about time you were her father?"

The king paled before an indignant flush hit his face. "Maybe instead of worrying about what I should do, you should get my daughter out of the predicament she's in only because you couldn't protect her in the first place."

The truth punched him in the nuts, but the pain only served to strengthen his resolve. "There's not a damn thing in the world that can stop me from saving Elle."

Ignoring protocol that demanded he wait until the king dismissed him, Dom turned and stalked across the asphalt to the other black sedan, where Major Bendtsen waited for him.

"As queen, she can't think about anything other than what's best for Elskov." The king's weakened, wheezy voice still had enough power to carry across the tarmac. "She's not for you."

Dom's step faltered. Old and ill, King Magnuz still knew how to slide a dagger. The king was right. Elle wasn't for him, he knew it, but that didn't change a damn thing. He yanked open the driver's side car door but stopped before sitting behind the wheel and looked back at the king, maybe for the last time.

"You're right. Elle's not mine, but that doesn't mean I won't always be hers."

And right now she needed him.

• • •

Elle woke up to a blue sky outside the window of the gilded prison that had been her childhood bedroom. One of the Hulk twins sat on an overstuffed chair, his bulky arms crossed and his eyes hidden behind a pair of sunglasses that he hadn't taken off since he'd escorted her to her mandated makeover. Now that wasn't creepy at all. She'd thought the poison GPS tracker cuff would have gotten Walther to let up on the goon squad. It hadn't.

"Good morning."

He grunted.

Well, so much for charming him with small talk to get him to conveniently look the other way. She flipped the thick comforter off and padded across the floor toward the connected bathroom, glad that she'd found a pair of pajama pants and a loose top waiting for her on top of the bed when the goon squad had locked her up in her tower bedroom for the night. The last thing she wanted was to give her captors a show. Shuffling across the thick carpet, her head still hazy with sleep, it took her a second to realize that Hulk One was following her.

She turned and nearly slammed into his concrete slab of a body. "I'm going to the bathroom, and you're not coming with me."

Nothing from the giant.

"Come on. Do you think I'm going to try to flush myself?"

He might have breathed. It was hard to tell with his head so high up.

"Anyway, there's this." She waved her arm with the cuff. "I'm not going anywhere, but I would like to pee in private."

His mouth formed a hard line, but he gave her a curt nod before turning and walking back to his chair by the door.

Score. Elle didn't look back as she rushed across the room and didn't let out the breath she was holding until she closed the thick, oak bathroom door behind her. She hurried to the linen closet next to the shower and yanked open the door. Shoving aside the stack of plush, cream towels, she pressed her palm against the back of the closet and felt the wall give. It wasn't a *Scooby-Doo* door, but her ancestors were as paranoid as the chalet's architect. Like most castles of a certain age, there were concealed servants' passages hidden between the walls at Elskov Castle. Now all she had to do was get rid of the stupid cuff.

Turning, she caught sight of a blonde out of the corner of her eye and squeaked in surprise before realizing she was looking at herself in the mirror. The makeover team hadn't been chatty or even the least bit friendly, but they'd done a great job taking her from her Nancy Drew strawberry blond back to the practically platinum she'd been since birth. Her brown contacts were gone, too, leaving her with the bright blue eyes that matched her father's.

Fury sizzled to the forefront again.

Her father was alive.

How in the fuck had he hidden that from her for all these years? How had he never reached out? How had he left her alone? Not that it mattered. He was as good as dead to her now anyway. She didn't know where he was, and he'd refused to even speak to her on the phone before the Fjende attacked the chalet. He couldn't have made his feelings more clear. Whatever she'd been to him at one time, she wasn't anymore. She stomped over to the shower and turned the knobs with shaking hands, letting the water rush over her arm before grabbing the soap.

"Taking a shower," she hollered over her shoulder as she worked up a good lather.

Using the soap as a lubricant, she tried to slide her hand through the cuff. Metal scraped against her tender flesh, pressing against the bone in her palm. Pain shot up her arm, and she clamped her jaws shut tight to keep from screaming, but she continued to pull her arm back as she pushed the metal cuff forward. The damn thing wouldn't go.

She sat back and sucked in a deep breath, her hand throbbing in agony and panic creeping up with stronger and surer steps with each heartbeat. The temptation to whack her arm against the porcelain tub until either the ceramic or the cuff's locked clasp cracked had her crazy eyed. But she couldn't. Sure, Walther could have been lying about toxin spraying from the cuff if she broke the clasp, but did she really want to risk it? No. She had to be smart. Inhaling a deep breath, she looked around the bathroom, looking for something, anything, that could help.

That's when she noticed the small, thin, square box in a basket by the sink. The label read: SHOWER CAP. The makeover mavens must have left it to protect the dye job. She grabbed the box and ripped it open, pulled out the cap, and tested the plastic covering and tight elastic band that went around it. Oh, that baby wasn't a cheap, flimsy shower cap. This was the industrial, beauty salon, means-business kind that would keep everything out. It would work. It had to. She didn't have another choice.

The idea gave her the heebie-jeebies, but desperate times called for putting a shower cap over your face. Eyeballing the silver clasp, she gauged just how much force she'd need to pop it. It would take work, but it wasn't impossible. After all, the threat wasn't in the difficulty but what would happen after.

She dug through the cabinets until found a flashlight and tucked it into the pocket of her pajama pants, then searched until she found something that would work on the cuff—narrow, pointed hair scissors. Weighing them in her palm, she tested the balance. They were quality craftsmanship, which would make things easier.

Steam from the shower filled the room, and a droplet of sweat slid down her neck. The last time she'd been in a steamy bathroom, she'd walked out to find Dom waiting for her. Her knees gave out, and her ass met the closet toilet lid with a hard *thunk*. If she closed her eyes, she could still feel his hands on her and hear the rough whisper of her name on his lips. Her throat tightened, and tears pricked her eyes. She squeezed her eyes shut and pictured Walther instead of Dom, let the anger boil and drown the grief. Dealing with that would come later.

Now she needed to focus on taking back her crown.

She pulled the shower cap on so it covered her face instead of her hair and secured the elastic, triple-checking that the elastic was secure. Each breath brought the thick plastic up against her nostrils. Each exhale made the air inside the covering thick and humid. She held her breath.

God, if there was any other way…but there isn't.

Without giving herself time for second thoughts, she took the hair scissors, slipped the tip through the small opening in the cuff's clasp as far as it would go, and twisted until it snapped. A white mist sprayed from the diamond as the cuff fell off her wrist, landing with a clank against the tile floor.

Walther hadn't been lying.

For a second, Elle couldn't move. Then the adrenaline kicked in, and she dashed across the bathroom, pushed her way to the back of the linen closet, secured the door, and shoved against the false wall. It gave. She stumbled into the darkness, her lungs burning. Taking the barest amount of time to press the wall back in place, she hurried down the cobweb-lined hall, getting as far as she could before releasing her breath and inhaling the clean, if stale, air.

Step one, done. Now to find Walther before he found her.

It was obvious from the cobweb cities visible in the pale light of her flashlight that no one used the servants' hallways much anymore, if at all. Still, she kept her eyes peeled for security cameras as she hustled through the dimly lit halls.

Left. Right. Left again. She hadn't been inside these walls since she was a girl, but playing defend the castle in them had been one of her favorite games growing up. Another few feet and there'd be another turn and then, finally, another door. She'd end up outside her father's chambers, near his private balcony overlooking the inner courtyard garden. At that point, it was a simple case of sneaking down and mixing in with the crowd no doubt already starting to gather in the garden for the Kronig. The pajamas would make her stand out in the formally dressed crowd, but she'd learned long ago that the key to any situation was to brazen her way through with her chin held high.

She turned the corner. There it was. Daylight peeked out through the small space between the door and the wall. The knob felt cool against her palm as she turned it and slowly inched the door open. A cool, fresh breeze tickled her nose and brought the sound of voices into the hall. But they weren't talking. They were…singing. She opened the door enough to confirm she'd come out by the garden as expected and peeked out to make sure no one was in the mezzanine leading to the king's chambers. Confirming the coast was clear, she gave in to the draw of the song.

She stuck to the shadows but came near enough to the balcony overlooking the garden to get a look at the children's choir singing the folk song that was the unofficial Elskov anthem. It was a love song about star-crossed lovers who were separated by distance and a bitter family feud but who managed to sneak off and make a home on a barren island. Their love turned the island into a paradise, and that paradise become Elskov. Children sang it in school. Adults raised their glasses in pubs as they sang it together. Often at weddings, newlyweds walked out of the church to an instrumental version.

Pursing her lips together, she closed her eyes and for a moment allowed herself to imagine walking out of the national cathedral with Dom as a violinist played the song. It was a pretty dream that ripped apart her insides. It couldn't have happened, and now it never would. Swallowing past the emotion, she opened her eyes and began to turn to—

An arm locked around her waist, jerking her back into the shadows, and a hand clamped tight over her mouth.

"You shouldn't be out wandering around, Your Highness," Walther whispered against her ear, evil clinging to his every word. "I see we're going to have to get you through the day using the power of chemistry. I have just the right drug to make you the perfect, pliant princess for the Kronig coronation ceremony." He buried his face in her hair and inhaled. "Of course, with any luck it will have worn off by the time I have you tonight. I like it when women try to fight back."

Good, because that's exactly what he was about to get. Recalling Dom's advice in the training room, she stomped down as hard as she could on Walther's instep. His hold on her loosened just enough that she could throw her head back and smash the back of her skull against his nose. The sound of bone cracking bounced across the high ceiling, and something wet sprayed the back of her neck.

"Bitch," Walther said, his voice quiet and weirdly muffled because of his broken nose but no less dangerous for it. "You'll pay for that."

His hand went from her mouth to her throat, his fingers curling around her windpipe and squeezing hard enough to make black spots appear in her vision. She clawed at his iron hold but couldn't break loose. He kept his feet out of striking distance and kept her tucked close against him so she couldn't get in another head butt or other defensive hit. She tried to scream for help, but only a strangled whisper came out as her limbs grew heavy and her ears rang.

"Don't worry, little princess, you won't die...yet." He dragged her back toward an open door that led to the king's former chambers. "But you are about to learn an important lesson."

The Hulk twins appeared in her peripheral vision.

Oh, shit.

One replaced Walther, picking her up with a beefy arm while ensuring her silence with a hand over her mouth. Elle kicked. She punched. She gave it everything she had, but it wasn't enough.

Chapter Fifteen

Dom adjusted the comm unit disguised as an iPod earbud in his ear and approached the castle's servants' entrance. With his conservative suit and plastic ID badge identifying him as part of the sound crew, he was able to slip into the flow of additional help brought in for the Kronig. Their agent on guard duty waved him inside without checking Dom's black duffel, which was filled with guns and ammo.

Sticking with the crowd, he made his way through the twists and turns toward the gardens where the Kronig would be starting in an hour.

"Sir," the major's voice crackled in his ear. "The princess is on the loose."

He slipped into the supply closet and shut the door behind him. "What in the hell do you mean?"

"Just got the report. She ditched her guards. Whereabouts unknown."

The whole world slid from under Dom's feet, but it was just like her. The woman excelled at disrupting plans—good to see her talent worked against the bad guys, too. He couldn't help the proud grin that curled his lips upward.

"Get all eyes on this. I need a location, stat."

Knowing running around the castle like a madman wouldn't help, he unzipped his duffel and took out the shoulder holster. They had fifty agents in the castle at that moment. At least one would spot her, and if not, the major had already hacked into the castle's security feed and was feeding it into his facial recognition program. They'd have her location within a minute.

He tucked a nine-millimeter into the holster, pocketed extra ammo, and double-checked the five throwing knives secured in his suit jacket. Everything was in place. Now he needed a location.

"What the fuck, Bendtsen," he said into the comm unit as he squashed the empty duffel into a ball and shoved it behind a stack of toilet paper rolls. "I need that location."

"We've got eyes on her," the major said.

I'm coming for you, Elle.

"Location?" He was halfway out the supply closet door before the word was out of his mouth.

"East wing, second floor, near the balcony overlooking the inner garden where the Kronig will be held."

She was close. He ran up the stairs, taking them two at a time.

"I'm patching you in with the agent in place," the major said.

There was a loud static buzz, and then a second voice joined Bendtsen's.

"They're on the move, sir."

Fear grabbed hold of Dom's throat and squeezed. "Who's they?"

"Henriksen has her."

The head of the Fjende, a snake and sadist in his own right. Things had just gone from bad to way fucking worse.

"Is she hurt?"

"The target has her by the throat, and she's struggling."

Dom withdrew his gun as he approached the landing. "Do you have a clear shot?"

"Negative, but the mezzanine is deserted except for the princess and Henriksen," the agent said. "Shit. The guards just came out of the king's chamber. They're taking her inside."

Adrenaline surging through him, Dom sprinted up the last few stairs and burst through the door opening up to the mezzanine, right in time to see the door to the king's chamber click shut.

The agent, wearing a butler's uniform, joined him.

"The king's chamber is a camera-free zone," the major said through the comm unit. "We don't know what's waiting inside. It could be a trap."

"Doesn't matter," Dom said. "I'm going in."

• • •

Elle screamed against the palm slapped over her mouth and clawed at the iron band of an arm around her waist.

Walther checked his watch. "As amusing as this is to watch, we don't have time for it—anyway, no one can hear you in here." He opened up a black pouch sitting on the desk and withdrew a needle and a glass bottle filled with a blue liquid. "Don't worry, this won't turn you into a doll." He filled the syringe. "No, this makes you nice and calm, the perfect, pliant little princess."

The guard moved his hand from over her mouth to the top of her head and yanked it to the side, exposing her neck for his boss. Adrenaline rushed through her, making every nerve stand up and scream. *Not again.* If she had any hope of getting away from Walther, of not becoming his puppet queen and royal incubator, she had to avoid being drugged.

The Kronig might be her last chance to defy him in a public setting where he couldn't harm her, and she couldn't do that if he got that needle in her.

"You don't have to do that." Desperation made her voice shake.

His smile was anything but kind as he held up the needle, tapping against it to remove any air bubbles. "You're saying you'll cooperate without the narcotic?"

She nodded, desperate not to lose even this sliver of a chance.

"Hmm." He cocked his head and gave her a considering look before screwing up his lips and shaking his head. "Nope. I don't believe you."

The other Hulk twin clamped his massive hands down on her and held her still. The needle pricked her neck, and a river of fire surged through her veins. Drawing on every last bit of strength she had, Elle swung her arms upward, connecting with Walther's arm.

"Bitch," he yelled as the half-full needle fell to the floor.

She inhaled a sharp breath, but before she could exhale euphoria settled over her, wrapping the world in cotton-candy gauze. It was like she was floating outside her body, watching Walther's face turn splotchy and red with fury when he realized the syringe had broken and all the liquid had leaked out. The vicious slap he delivered across her face was a mere love tap. None of it mattered.

The door flew open, and Dom rushed through. Her Dom. She loved him so much, and he'd come for her. A lightness, practically blinding in its brightness, filled her, but it wasn't right. She knew the man firing a gun with deadly accuracy into the Hulk twins wasn't Dom.

Dom was dead.

Realization pierced the soft haze around her. She'd wanted him so badly that her mind had produced him, a cruel joke for a woman who still had choices but couldn't make the one she wanted most of all—to choose Dom.

Walther grabbed her hair, jerking her to a standing position so she was in front of him, a gun pressed to her temple. The imaginary Dom hesitated, his finger on the trigger of the gun in his hand. Her pulse barely registered an uptick. Still, seeing him and it not being him was more than she could bear. She didn't bother to hold back the tears. What did it matter? She'd lost everything when she'd lost Dom.

"Put the fucking gun down or I'll kill her," Walther said.

Both imaginary Dom and the stranger with him squatted slowly and put their guns on the floor.

"You're out of options, Henriksen," imaginary Dom said as he stood back up. "We've already rounded up the other Fjende leaders. Put the gun down, and you'll walk away alive."

"Not in this lifetime," Walther said. "Here's what's going to happen. You're going to stay right where you are, and in about ten seconds my men will be here and you'll be swinging from a rope by sunset."

"Elle," imaginary Dom said, his voice like a salve to her wounds. "Look at me."

She didn't have the strength not to pretend it was the real Dom, so she did. "I love you."

He smiled, but there was sadness in it. "Drop."

She didn't hesitate. She fell back on what she'd learned during their training sessions and let her knees go loose. In the same instant, a silver knife whistled over her head. A wild scream echoed in the room, and Walther fell the ground, the gun limp in his hand. The knife buried to the hilt in what used to be his right eye. The imaginary Dom rushed over, kicked the gun away, and gathered her in his arms and carried her to the other side of the room. Not letting go of her, he sat down on the edge of the bed.

Men dressed in fatigues stormed into the room, guns at

the ready.

"Call the doctor. I don't know what they gave her, but she's out of it," imaginary Dom told them.

They gave her a few quick glances but followed orders, leaving her alone with the man who couldn't be here. God, he smelled like the real thing. He felt like the real thing. If she'd had even a few more drops of that drug, she would have believed he was the real thing. She buried her face in his shoulder and wrapped her arms around him as if she could force a ghost to stay. "Don't go."

"I have to." He brushed a stray hair out of her face and tucked it behind her ear, his actions a soft kindness in comparison to the hard hurt of his words. Then he settled her down on the bed, laying her head on the pillow with utmost gentleness, his blue eyes shiny. "I can't be your future, so I have to be your past."

"I love you." It came out as a quiet whimper as the agony of losing him again ripped through the gossamer, drugged haze around her, leaving her shredded and miserable. "Don't leave me alone again."

He leaned down and took her face in his hands. His lips brushed against hers, a mere hint at the emotion swamping them both. The kiss wasn't a promise; it was a good-bye.

• • •

Mission accomplished. Now he needed to get the hell out of here before he couldn't. One foot in front of the other. It was Dom's turn to run. He pushed against the flow of people rushing toward the king's chamber, including a doctor carrying a black bag. He tapped the comm unit in his ear. "Status report."

"I'm on my way to the queen's chamber now," said Major Bendtsen. "The Fjende leaders are either in custody or dead."

"Alton?" He hurried down the stairs and toward the back entrance.

"Dead," the major said.

With the leadership decimated, the Fjende would crumble into dust. He'd make sure of it. They'd never threaten Elle again. "The media?"

"We're going to spin it as a failed assassination attempt on the princess prior to the Kronig. No one has any idea she's ever been gone."

"Good. I'll need you to make sure it stays that way." Simple and close enough to the truth to make the lie authentic. The major had chosen the cover story well, but his job wasn't done. Not even close. "She's going to need you, Major. Be the adviser she can count on. We stick to the original plan. I disappear, and you act as the queen's right hand as long as she needs you."

He stepped out the door and into the bright sunlight. There wasn't a cloud in the sky anymore. It was as if even Mother Nature was glad Elle was home.

"Sir, where are you going?"

"I'll find out when I get there." It would be a place where he could keep an eye on Elle and finish the job of putting the Fjende completely out of commission. He had to leave, but she'd never be alone again, not really. "Radio the pilot at the airfield and let him know to be ready to take off."

Dom crossed the lot to the black sedan he'd driven in from the airport, opened the door, and slid behind the wheel.

"You're not staying for the Kronig?" the major asked. "It's all you've cared about for the past ten years."

It had been until Princess Eloise turned out to be Elle. He'd tear the world apart for her, but it turned out the best thing he could do for her was rip out his own heart. In a few hours she'd be Elskov's queen, and queens didn't marry for love, unless you counted the love of country. They most definitely didn't marry commoners who weren't even citizens. She'd said she loved him. That was the one choice she couldn't make as queen.

"Good-bye, Major, it's been a pleasure." He turned the key in the ignition. "Watch over her."

Without waiting for a response, Dom yanked the comm unit out of his ear and dropped it out the car's window before pulling away and driving until the castle was only a dot in his rearview mirror.

• • •

Whatever shot the doctor had given Elle had done the trick. Twenty minutes later she was sitting up in bed, propped up by pillows and very nearly 100 percent herself. At least enough so that she'd kicked out everyone except Major Bendtsen.

He stood at attention at the foot of the bed, hands clasped behind his back looking every bit like the career military officer he was. Control. Determination. Power. No wonder Dom had picked him as his right-hand man. He was a force to be reckoned with…but so was she. And there was no way the man who'd rescued her could be anyone other than Dom. She'd woken up from the drugged haze knowing it with as much certainty as she knew the earth was round. Even though she already knew the answer, she had to ask. "Is he alive? Was that really Dom?"

The major hesitated for only a half second before his dark green eyes locked with hers. "Yes, Your Highness."

She sank back against the pillows and let out a relieved sigh. "How? I saw the chalet come down."

"It's a good thing his backup plans have backups." A rare grin from the major.

"Where is he now?" Because it sure as hell wasn't where he was supposed to be. Not after everything they'd been through.

"He's at the airport. He thought it best if he headed up the search for any remaining Fjende who may have fled Elskov."

Before she had a chance to question him further, the door opened and a man entered. His hair was gone, his body bent with age and pain, but there was no mistaking the blue eyes, because they were the same distinctive shade as her own.

He hesitated at the door for a moment before crossing over to what used to be his bed. The tip of his silver cane tapped against the stone floor with each step, each one emphasizing how much the man before her was a shadow of his former self. Thin. Pale. Broken. It was like looking into a carnival mirror reflection of the man her father had been. It broke her heart.

Slowly, he eased himself down until he sat next to her on the bed, the mattress barely dipping under his weight. "Look at you, Eloise. Your mother would be so proud."

Knowing he was alive was one thing—seeing him quite another. She didn't know whether to push him away or pull him close. She kinda wanted to do both. "How could you?"

Tears in his eyes, he took her hand in his frail, thin one. "At first it was because I thought it was the best way to keep you safe until you were ready to come back home and do what needed to be done for Elskov. Then my body began to reject the transplants I needed after the assassination attempt. One by one, they started to shut down. What kind of father would make his child watch him die twice?"

The image of him bleeding all over the castle steps flashed in her mind. That was how she had always pictured him. Not the games of tag in the formal gardens or the late-night discussions about Elskovian history in the library or the songs they used to make up and sing on the way to royal appearances. She'd been so focused on the bad that she'd blocked out the good. Well, now she had a second chance with him, and she wasn't going to lose it.

Glancing down at their intertwined hands, she swallowed past the emotion making her throat tight. "Will you stay in Elskov?"

Sadness and regret dimmed the blue of his eyes. "You know that can't happen. In a few hours, you'll be queen. Those loyal to the Fjende would have eaten up the sweet seventeen-year-old girl you were, but they've got a much stronger enemy in the woman you've become. You are Elskov's best choice." He squeezed her hand. "That doesn't mean I don't want to be part of your life. If you'll allow it, I'd like to be as much a part of your life as I can. Believe me, if I could go back and do it differently, I would. I was so focused on my duty to Elskov that it blinded me to my duty to my daughter. It is my greatest failing. Can you ever forgive me?"

"I shouldn't." Her voice shook.

"I understand." He started to get up.

She refused to let go of his hand. "But I do."

He wrapped his arms around her, and they clung to each other as she let the tears she'd been holding back fall freely— they both did. He wasn't perfect, but he was her father, and he'd done what he'd thought was the best thing for her and for Elskov. She couldn't hold on to the anger that had twisted her up, not when she was making the same choice when it came to Dom.

He pulled back and wiped the tears from her cheeks before standing. "I'll be watching the Kronig from the jet. I have to go back to Spain. If I stay here any longer, I could ruin everything for you."

"I understand." She stood, her legs a little wobbly but not enough to stop her from walking her father to the door.

He paused, his hand on the knob. "You're more like your mother every day. She was strong and dedicated to Elskov, but she understood the importance of balance when it came to royal duty and love. I hope you'll follow her example as a ruler rather than mine."

"You mean Dom." Her heart fluttered at the taste of his name on her lips.

Her father nodded. "He didn't have the choice to tell you about me. No one knows what that's like more than you. Don't let the crown and your duty blind you like it did me. He loves you."

"How do you know?"

Her father gave her an indulgent smile. "Don't you?" He walked through the door, a wall of guards surrounding him and blocking him from view.

Elle closed the door and surveyed the room she'd never thought she'd occupy in a country she'd never thought she'd see again. Being queen wasn't a choice, it was her destiny, her duty, but it wasn't all she was. She was still Elle, and she wasn't alone anymore. She flung open the door.

"Major Bendtsen," she called.

He appeared immediately. "Yes, Your Royal Highness."

"I have a mission for you."

• • •

Dom glanced down at his watch. The jet should have taken off ten minutes ago. Instead it was frozen on the airstrip, and damn his mutinous heart, he was more than a little glad to still be breathing the same air as Elle, knowing that as soon as the plane took off he'd never see her again.

The pilot opened the cockpit door and headed toward Dom.

"What's the holdup?" Dom asked.

"Sir, you might want to look out the window."

Annoyed at the cryptic response, he shoved up the shade covering the window next to his seat—a line of Humvees bearing the royal seal surrounded the jet. Fear twisted his heart in two. Elle. The Fjende. He should have stayed. He should have watched over her.

Major Bendtsen got out of one of the Humvees, a bullhorn in his hand.

"The princess requests your presence at the Kronig. She says..." Bendtsen paused, a smile curling his normally taciturn expression into one of humor. "One kidnapping deserves another."

Chapter Sixteen

The garden was filled with Elskovian aristocracy, dripping with diamonds and the finest bespoke tailored tuxedos, drinking champagne in honor of the country's new queen, but the one man Elle wanted to see wasn't there. Standing on the dais, the Elskovian crown firmly atop her newly blond hair, she listened with half an ear to a foreign diplomat paying his respects.

Murmurs of surprise lifted above the chatter, drawing her attention toward the entrance guarded by men in full royal dress uniforms of blue and silver. Thirty men and women in black fatigues walked through, looking as deadly as she knew them to be. Some she recognized from the chalet. Others had been passing figures in the crazy moments after Dom had burst into her room and killed the Hulk twins and Walther. The Resistance, her guardian angels watching over her even when she hadn't known they'd been there.

The crowd parted for them as they made their way to the dais, a silent testament to the bravery and determination of her people. They'd fought for a decade to restore the monarchy and return her to Elskov. She owed them her loyalty and her life. Major Bendtsen stood at the head of the line, his face a neutral mask, but Dom wasn't anywhere in the group.

Her stomach folded up inside itself. She'd been too late. He was gone.

Another rustle of chatter, then Dom walked past the royal guards and into the garden. Even though he was dressed in his personal uniform of a dark blue suit that set off the crisp blue of his eyes and his light blond hair, he couldn't disguise the Viking warrior hidden inside. He'd fought for her. Now she'd fight for him.

As soon as he joined the other Resistance fighters in front of her, she withdrew the ceremonial sword from the silver sheath slung around her waist.

"Ladies and gentlemen of Elskov, before you stand the bravest among us. Today marks a new beginning for me as your queen and for Elskov as a country, thanks to the actions of these dedicated few who sprang into action when I was threatened."

There was more, so much more that they'd done, but she'd agreed with the major to stick with the cover story of an assassination attempt instead of the whole truth of ten years of lies and royal impersonators. "In honor of their courage and valor, I bestow upon these citizens of Elskov the rank of silver knights. It has been centuries since our fair country has had a council of knights watching over her, and we are in good hands with these protectors."

Starting at the opposite end from Dom, she walked down the line of Resistance fighters, tapping each on the shoulders with the sword and granting them admittance into the circle of aristocracy. When she got to the major, she paused.

"Of course, every council needs a leader. There is none I can imagine as being a better one than you, Major Bendtsen, the Earl of Moad." The title came with a country estate north of the capital and the responsibility of being in charge of the country's security.

Her hand shook as she lowered the sword to her side and walked the final two steps to stand in front of Dom. While the others had bowed before her, he stood tall and powerful with those thick lips that begged to be kissed, sucked, devoured, and the muscular body of a man who could stand up to any challenge and win. She could look at him all day and never grow tired. Even in front of all of these people, she couldn't help but drink in her fill. His blue-eyed gaze clashed with hers, and he gave her a slow wink that made her thighs clench.

"Queen Eloise." He executed a perfect bow before standing straight again. "That won't work on me. I'm not a citizen."

Taking a deep breath, she squared her shoulders. They'd had their Roman Holiday, but she wasn't about to let him gallantly walk away like the reporter had done. This was their destiny, and together they'd seize it.

"True, but being queen has its privileges—conferring citizenship and titles being one of them. It hasn't happened since my great-grandmother Queen Margriet bestowed the honor on the man who would later become her king."

He raised an eyebrow, cocky as always. "And is that what you had in mind for me?"

"Yes," she said.

"I'm afraid I cannot accept such an honor." Dom shook his head. "That's not the title I want."

The world dropped from beneath her feet.

• • •

The crowd gasped, but Dom ignored them. They didn't matter to him. Only Elle mattered. She was the only one who really ever had, and she looked like she was about to faint or chop off his head with the sword in her white-knuckled grip. He needed to get talking fast, or she just might pick the more old-school route of the two choices.

"You see, I'm in love with a girl who wants me to wear casual clothes and likes to challenge my every move. She's stubborn and impulsive and even tried to shoot me."

Her lips twitched, and her death grip on the sword loosened and she sheathed it. "It was just the once, and you deserved it."

Soft chuckles from the glitterati surrounded them.

"You see, I'm not in love with the queen." He took her free hand in his, that familiar spark whenever he touched her turning his dick to stone. "I'm in love with Elle."

Realization dawned in her eyes, and her cheeks turned that distinctive rose that was all Elle. "And she's in love with you."

"You always have choices, Elle, even now that you're queen." He dropped down to one knee not because she was his queen, but because she was the woman he loved, worshipped, and adored. "Will you, Elle, choose me, Dom, not as a member of the Resistance, but as the man you love?"

For too long his life had revolved around revenge, around keeping control. He'd had no idea it could be different, it could be more until he'd kidnapped the woman who'd turned out to be the love of his life. She'd changed everything.

"Elle, I have billions in the bank, people at my disposal, and countries I can influence, but the only title I want is husband—to be your husband. Will you marry me?"

Tears made the blue of her eyes brighter, but her smile was anything but sad. "Yes."

Dom stood and wrapped his arms around her, aligning their bodies, and brought his mouth down to hers in a kiss that promised she'd never be alone again. It wasn't the beginning for them. It was forever.

Epilogue

Two weeks later Major Lucas Bendtsen got out of his BMW roadster parked in front of the three-story manor house and surveyed his new home. The title of Earl of Moad had come with a country estate on one hundred acres of prime land. The manor house stood on a fjord overlooking the North Sea crashing against the rocks. It wasn't the bright lights of Harbor City or the constant crush of people in London, but he could get used to it. After growing up on the streets of the capital and doing whatever it took to survive, he'd learned the hard way that he could get used to anything and rise above it. The millions in his bank account proved that.

A gentleman spymaster, that's what the addict's son had grown into, with a country house and a title. An aristocrat. His mother would have died of surprise if the needle hadn't gotten to her already.

His phone vibrated in his suit pocket, a reminder that while he might be lord of the manor, he was also the head of Elskov's silver knights, an elite intelligence and fighting arm answerable only to the queen herself.

He took out his cell and glanced at the caller ID. It was the agent heading up Operation Family Jewels. Whoever had picked that name deserved a kick in his.

Lucas pressed the talk button. "Yes."

"Sir, we have her. She's on her way to you now."

Adrenaline spiked in his system, and he began pacing in front of the manor house. "Does she know why?"

"Negative. She thinks you are interested in having her design a jeweled family crest befitting of your new station in life."

God. That made him sound like a total knob. People actually did that? He shook his head. "And the brother?"

"He's in custody."

"Good. Don't let him go." The scumbag deserved a nice long stay behind bars for bringing two kilos of cocaine into Elskov, but the asshole was still useful, so instead he was sitting in comfort in a safe house on the isolated south shore. "He's our best leverage to get her to do what we need."

"Are you sure this is the best plan? There are risks in blackmailing the daughter of one of Europe's most notorious crime bosses with a side business as an arms dealer."

Lucas stopped in his tracks. This wasn't the best plan. It was the only plan. They had one shot, and he wasn't about to let the sexy little jewelry designer get away without agreeing to his terms. The number of men who ended up the victims of jewel theft, murdered during a robbery, or never heard from again after tangling with the mobster's daughter was in dispute, but fifty was probably in the conservative range of possibility. The only question was did the bombshell lure the men into her father's web or do the dirty deeds herself?

"You've read the same reports as I have," he said, not bothering to keep the icy clip out of his voice. "Walther Henriksen's son came out of hiding just long enough to put the word out that he wants to buy enough weapons to take over a small country. Three guesses about which country that is. Forcing Ruby MacIntosh to be our mole in her father's operation means we can stop an attack before it happens."

"Just be sure you don't fall under her spell. She has a reputation."

"So do I." He grinned. If the man on the other end of the phone could have seen it, he would have taken three steps back. "Be at my office at six tomorrow morning for a briefing. This operation is a go."

Lucas hung up the phone and turned toward the mile-long driveway. Ruby MacIntosh would arrive within minutes, and then, one way or another, her life would change forever. He'd see to it.

About the Author

When Avery Flynn isn't writing about alpha heroes and the women who tame them, she is desperately hoping someone invents the coffee IV drip. She has three slightly wild children, loves a hockey-addicted husband, and has a slight shoe addiction. Find out more about Avery on her website, follow her on Twitter, like her Facebook page or friend her Facebook profile. Also, if you figure out how to send Oreos through the internet, she'll be your best friend for life. Contact her at avery@averyflynn.com. She'd love to hear from you.

Discover more category romance titles from Entangled Indulgence...

THE GREEK'S STOWAWAY BRIDE
a novel by Alexia Adams

Hoping to make it to North Africa to free her uncle, Egyptian heiress Rania Ghalli stows away on the yacht of Greek millionaire Demetri Christodoulou. But when Egyptian agents board the boat, she can either jump overboard...or claim she's Demetri's new bride. Demetri needs a wife to complete a land purchase so he agrees to play along—*if* she'll agree to a *real* marriage. But keeping the vivacious heiress out of his heart will be a lot harder than keeping her on his ship...

THE PRINCE'S RUNAWAY LOVER
a *Men of the Zodiac* novel by Robin Covington

Crown Prince Nicholas Lytton is about to become the king. And the best way to secure his crown is to do the unthinkable—find a queen. While Isabel Reynolds works in the palace gardens, she has no desire to draw the attention of the way-too-flirty, would-be king. The promise of love would only end in disaster. Because while Isabel may be able to catch a king, her secrets would only destroy him...

SLEEPING WITH THE OPPOSITION
a *Bad Boy Bosses* novel by J.K. Coi

Leo Markham has everything a man could want. Money. Power. Respect. But there's only one thing he *needs*—Bria. Trouble is, she's determined to move on, despite the breathtaking passion still between them. Sure, he's made mistakes, but he'll make her forgive him. He can't lose the only woman who's ever had his heart.